Mia Couto was born in Mozambique in 1955. When his country became independent in 1975, Couto interrupted his studies to become a journalist and newspaper editor. Later, he resumed his studies, and is now an environmental biologist. He has published poetry, short stories and a number of novels. His work has been widely recognised in the Portuguese-speaking world, and has been translated into a number of European languages. *Under the Frangipani*, *The Last Flight of the Flamingo*, *A Sleepwalking Land* and *A River Called Time* have all been published in English translation by Serpent's Tail.

Praise for Mia Couto's novels

Under the Frangipani

'This is an original and fresh tale quite unlike anything else I have read from Africa. I enjoyed it very much' Doris Lessing

'To read Mia Couto is to encounter a peculiarly African sensibility, a writer of fluid, fragmentary narratives…a remarkable novel' *New Statesman*

'Blending history, death, and a uniquely African flavour of magic realism, *Under the Frangipani* is a powerful and trenchant evocation of life in a society traumatised by decades of war and poverty' *New Internationalist*

'Couto's tale unfolds on two levels: first, as a mystery story, for the fantastic confessions generate a "whodunnit" suspense; more demandingly as a thematic puzzle' *TLS*

'Anything but an everyday whodunit…it is a novel which forces the reader to question preconceived notions, to take a second look at assumptions that normally go unnoticed and to try to look at the world with fresh, unspoiled eyes' *Worldview*

The Last Flight of the Flamingo

'Couto is considered the most prominent of the younger generation of writers in Portuguese-speaking Africa. In his novels, Couto passionately and sensitively describes everyday life in poverty-stricken Mozambique…ingenious literature – gripping and mysterious, yet never without humour' *Guardian*

'UN officials, the prostitute, the bureaucrat; carriers of ancient lore and modern ideas chat and clash in this gnomic, comic parable of change in Africa, deftly translated by David Brookshaw' *Independent*

'Couto adroitly captures the chaos and comedy of an abrupt and externally imposed shift in ideologies. No one gets off lightly… The narrative shifts nimbly through a range of registers, from supple wordplay to lyricism' *London Review of Books*

'A wry, poignant fable about any society lost in translation' *New York Times*

'A showcase for Couto's extraordinary vision… an impressive novel' *Miami Herald*

'The book has fierce vitality… The narrator's friendship with the hapless investigator Massimo is touching and complex… real eloquence' *Time Out*

'A wonderful mix of magical realism and wordplay that has a similar tone to Marquez at his best. Couto writes in an idiom all his own that feels authentically African' *Ink*

'A portrait of its milieu: steeped in folkways, awash in petty tyranny and corruption. The book is also a showcase for Couto's extraordinary vision. Even in translation, his prose is suffused with striking images…an impressive novel' *Washington Post*

A Sleepwalking Land

'The story is spare and achingly universal. It draws on a timeless tradition of oral storytelling while firmly rooting itself in the terrible reality of life in a war zone' *New Internationalist*

'A colourful, arresting tale' *Spectator*

'Abstract and figurative, this is very much a fable for adults, and a spirited revolt against the brutal reality of war' *The Works*

'A poignant tale of war and the emptiness it leaves behind' *Big Issue*

Under the Frangipani

Mia Couto

Translated by David Brookshaw

This translation is supported by the
Portuguese Institute for Book and Libraries

Funded by the Arts
Council of England

Thanks also to the Portuguese Trust

First published as A Varanda do Frangipani in 1996 by Editorial Caminho, SA, Lisboa

First published in this edition in 2008 by Serpent's Tail
First published in 2001 by Serpent's Tail,
an imprint of Profile Books Ltd
3A Exmouth House
Pine Street
London EC1R OJH
website: www.serpentstail.com

ISBN: 978 1 84668 676 4

Typeset at Neuadd Bwll, Llanwrtyd Wells

Printed and bound in Great Britain by CPI Bookmarque,
Croydon, Surrey, CRO 4TD
10 9 8 7 6 5 4 3 2

Mixed Sources
Product group from well-managed
forests and other controlled sources
www.fsc.org Cert no. TT-COC-002227
© 1996 Forest Stewardship Council

Contents

White body, black soul

When I first met Mia Couto some fifteen years ago, I was surprised. I had read some of his writing and was quite sure that he was an African. But he wasn't. Or, to be exact: he was indeed an African, but a white man who had been born in Africa – in Mozambique – to European parents. I need to emphasise this because one of the most challenging things about Mia Couto's work is how profoundly it manifests an African sense of how a good story should be told. He confirms that skin colour never really explains a person's cultural, artistic or philosophical dimensions. Mia Couto can be said to be a white man with an African soul.

In African storytelling, there is first of all an absolute challenge to the chronological narrative. There are, for example, in Couto's work apparent detours into the life-story of the various characters that turn out to be necessary 'because things begin even before they happen'. Couto also appears to be a restless drifter between the past and the present, which is true to the way in which African storytellers make a less rigid distinction between the past and the present than writers in the West. He walks in and out of the door that separates dreams and visions from reality. Indeed, the question 'What is reality?' is buried under the words as a constant subtext. As well as this, Couto explores the African spirit world, which not only allows the dead to meet and even inhabit the living, but also accepts metamorphosis between people and other living creatures because they are interrelated. By meshing the richness of African beliefs, traditions and customs into the Western framework of the novel, he creates a mysterious and surreal epic that makes the reader keep wondering: where is he taking me now?

Henning Mankell

Chaka, founder of the Zulu empire, to his murderers
You will never govern this land.
It will only ever be governed by the swallows from the
other side of the sea,
the ones with transparent ears . . .
cited by H. Junod

Mozambique: this huge balcony overlooking the Indian
Ocean . . .
Eduardo Lourenço on his departure from Maputo in 1995

1 The dead man's dream

I am the dead man. If I had a cross or a slab of marble, the name Ermelindo Mucanga would feature on it. But I passed away along with my name nearly two decades ago. For years, I was an esteemed inhabitant of life, a person of respectable origin. Though I was an upright citizen while alive, my death was inglorious. My burial lacked both ceremony and tradition. There wasn't even anyone to bend my knees. People are supposed to leave the world just as they entered it, curled up as if saving on space. The dead should be humble enough not to take up much of the earth. But I wasn't given a small grave. My resting place stretched from one end to the other of my whole length. No one unclasped my hands as I grew cold. I crossed over into death with my fists clenched, summoning curses upon the living. And to make matters worse, they didn't turn my face towards the Nkuluvumba Mountains. We Mucangas have obligations towards times gone by. Our dead gaze at the spot where the first woman jumped the moon, causing her belly and her soul to take on its roundness.

I wasn't just denied a proper funeral. Their negligence

went even further: as I had no other possessions, they buried me with my saw and hammer. They shouldn't have done that. Metal should never be allowed into a tomb. Iron takes longer to rust away than a dead man's bones. And what's worse, a shiny object attracts a curse. With my tools by my side, I risk being one of those dead people who wreak havoc on the world.

All these upsets happened because I didn't die in my rightful place. I was working far from my home town. I was a carpenter at the Portuguese fort of São Nicolau, which was then being restored. I left the world just as my country was about to become free. That was the funny thing: my country was being born, dressed up in its flag, and I was being lowered into the ground, banished from the light. Maybe it was just as well, for I didn't have to witness wars and other disasters.

As they didn't assign me a proper funeral, I became a ghost, one of those souls who wander from somewhere to nowhere. Seeing as I hadn't been given a formal send-off, I ended up as a dead man who couldn't find his death. I shall never be elevated to the position of an ancestor, someone well and truly dead and gone for good, with a right to be invoked and cherished by the living. I'm one of those dead men who are still attached to life by their umbilical cord. I belong to the fellowship of those who are unremembered. But I don't go around sowing confusion among the living. I accepted the captivity of my grave, I lay down quietly as befits the dead.

It helped that they had buried me near a tree. Where I come from, a *maroola* is chosen. Or a kapok tree. But the only tree here in the fort is a skinny little frangipani. That's where they buried me. The sweet-scented flowers of the frangipani fall over the place where I lie. So many that I now smell of their petals. Is it worth sweetening me up like this? For nowadays, only the wind can smell me. No one else cares about me. I've long become resigned to it. Even those folk who can always be found in cemeteries, what do they know about the dead? Fears, shadows and darkness. Even a veteran of death like me can count wisdom on the fingers of my hand. Dead people don't dream much, that much I can tell you. They only dream on rainy nights. At other times, they are the ones who are dreamed. I, who never had anyone to spare me a moment of memory, who am I dreamt by? The tree. Only the frangipani devotes a few nightly thoughts to me.

The frangipani occupies the terrace of a colonial fort. This terrace has witnessed much history. Slaves, ivory and cloth were all shipped out through it. From its stonework, Portuguese cannons blazed against Dutch ships. Towards the end of colonial times, it was decided to build a prison there to shut away the revolutionaries who were fighting the Portuguese. After independence, it was turned into a makeshift refuge for old people. With their arrival, the place went into decline. Then civil war came, producing a harvest of death. But the fighting took place far from the fort. When the war ended, the refuge remained, unclaimed by anyone as an inheritance. Here, time was drained of its colour, everything starched by silence and emptiness. In this dissonant place, like a snake's shadow, I established myself as an unlikely ancestor.

Until one day, I was awoken by a thumping and
shaking. Someone was interfering with my grave. I
thought it might be my neighbour, the mole, sightless so
as to see in the dark. But it wasn't that burrowing
creature. My sacred ground was being abused by picks and
shovels. What was it that spurred those people on, causing
my death to come alive? I pried into their conversation
and understood: the governors wanted to turn me into a
national hero. They were wrapping me in glory. Rumours
were even spreading that I had died in battle fighting the
colonial oppressor. Now, they wanted my mortal remains.
Or rather, my immortal remains. They needed a hero, but
not just any old one. They wanted one of my particular
race, tribe and region. To satisfy discord and placate the
aggrieved. They wanted to put race on display, to peel off
the skin and show the fruit. The nation needed a stage. Or
was it the other way round? From being needy, I became
needed. That's why they were digging up my burial
ground, right there, nice and deep, in the yard of the
fortress. When I realised what was happening, I didn't
know what to do.

I was never a man of many ideas, but nor am I so dead
that I can't get my tongue round words. I had to undo
their deception. Otherwise I'd never get any peace. If I
had died, it was in order to become a lone shadow. It
wasn't for parties, for loud sing-songs, for drum dances.
Apart from this, a hero is like a saint. No one really and
truly loves him. He is remembered in times of personal
grief and national affliction. I wasn't loved when I was
alive, and I didn't need this intrusion now.

I remembered the story of the chameleon. Everyone knows the tale: God sent the chameleon to bear the message of eternity. The creature dallied in giving men the secret of everlasting life. He dallied so much that God had time to change his mind, and send another messenger with counter-tidings. Well, I am a back-to-front messenger: I take messages from men to the gods. I'm taking too long to deliver my tidings. By the time I get to where the gods dwell, they will have received untidings from someone else.

What's certain is that I had no desire to be a hero after my death. That award was to be avoided, whatever the cost. But what could I do, as a ghost with neither law nor respect on my side? I even thought of reappearing in the body I had when I was alive, the body of a youth. I would double back through my navel and come out the other side, a ghost of flesh and bone, with a voice that could be heard by other mortals. But a spirit that reoccupies its former body risks mortal dangers: when it touches or is touched, it's enough to send hearts thumping backwards and sow fatal consequences.

I consulted my pet anteater. Is there anyone who doesn't know of the powers of this scaly beast, the *halakavuma*, as we call it? Well, this mammal lives with the dead. It descends from the heavens during the rainy season. It falls to earth to spread news to the world, to the ancestors of the future. I've got an anteater with me, just as I had a dog when I was alive. It curls up by my feet, and I use it as a pillow. I asked my *halakavuma* what I should do.

—*Don't you want to be a hero?*

But a hero of what, beloved of whom? Now that the country is a harvest of ruins, why do they call for me, a humble carpenter? The anteater began to prey upon my interest.

—*Wouldn't you like to be alive again?*

—*No, I wouldn't. Not in the state my country is in.*

The anteater turned round on itself. Was it following its rear end, or tuning its voice so that I could hear it better? For the creature doesn't talk to all and sundry. It drew itself up on its hind legs, like a real person trying to rouse my interest. Pointing towards the courtyard of the fortress, it said

—*Look around you, Ermelindo. Even amongst these ruins, wild flowers have taken root.*

—*I don't want to go back there.*

—*But it will forever be your garden: there between those wounded stones and wasteland blooms.*

The scaly creature's meanderings began to irritate me. I reminded him that it was advice I wanted, a solution. The *halakavuma* assumed a solemn tone and said

—*You, Ermelindo, you should relive your death.*

Die again? As if it wasn't hard enough to leave life the first time! If my family's tradition was anything to go by, it would surely be an impossible task. My grandfather, for instance, has lasted an infinity. He wasn't dead yet for sure. The old man slept with his legs spread out from his trunk, next to dangerous foliage. By doing this, he tempted snake bites. In small doses, their poison increases our vitality. Anyway, that's what he used to tell us. And life seemed to prove him right: he was ever more full of strength and energies. The *halakavuma* was like my grandfather, as persistent as a pendulum. The creature pressed his case.

—*Choose one who's about to peg out.*

Isn't the surest place a mamba's nest? I should emigrate into the body of one about to die. Hitch a ride on another death and dissolve into the birth of its end. It didn't seem hard. In the refuge there would be no shortage of people on their last legs.

—*You mean, I'm going to ghost myself via someone else's body?*

—*You'll take the form of a* shipoco, *a night spirit.*

—*Let me think,* I said.

Deep down, the decision had already been taken. I was only pretending to be master of my own will. That night, I was already on my way to becoming a *shipoco*. In other words, I was turning into a night spirit, travelling in someone else's shape. If I were to return to my own body, I would only be visible from the front. Seen from the back, I would merely be a hollow hole, a piece of vacant emptiness. But I was going to occupy another man's body. I was in transit from the prison of my grave to the prison of a body. I was forbidden to touch life, to feel the wind's breath directly. From my little corner, I would see the world through a gauze, translucently. My only advantage would be in the matter of time. For the dead, time follows in yesterday's tracks. For them, there are no surprises.

At first, I still had my doubts: was the *halakavuma* telling me the truth? Or had he been away from the world for so long that he was making it up? He hadn't touched the earth's surface for years, his nails were growing round and round in numerous coils. If even his paws yearned for the ground, why should his head not be full of raving lunacies? But soon I began to busy myself thinking about my journey back to the world of the living.

I looked forward to it so much that my dreams were even devoid of rain or night. What did I dream? I dreamt they were burying me in the time-honoured way, as required by our beliefs. I was dying resting on my haunches, my chin perched on my knees. That's how I was lowered into the earth, and my body came to rest on sand dug from a termite mound. Live sand, colonized by the restless. Then they covered me with sand gently, as if they were dressing a child. They didn't use spades. Only their hands did the work. When the sand reached my eyes, they stopped. Then they planted acacia shoots all around me. Everything ready to burst into flower. And to summon the rain, they covered me with damp earth. And that's how I learnt that when we are alive we tread the ground, but when we are dead we are trodden by it.

And I dreamt still more: after my death, all the women in the world slept out in the open. It wasn't just the widows who were forbidden to seek shelter, as is normal in our beliefs. No. It was as if all the women had lost a husband in me. All were tainted by my death. Grief spread through every village like a thick blanket of mist. Lamps lit up the corn, trembling hands holding their crucible of fire passed along the rows of maize. They were protecting the fields from the evil eye.

Next day, hardly had I awoken than I began to shake the *halakavuma*. I wanted to know whose body I was going to occupy.

—*It's someone who hasn't arrived yet.*

—*Which someone?*

—*It's someone from outside. He's arriving tomorrow.* Then, he added —*It's a pity I didn't remember earlier. A week before, and everything would have been over and done with by now. Just a few days ago, a bigwig was killed, right here in the refuge.*

—*What bigwig?*

—*The director of the refuge. He was shot dead.*

It was because of this murder that a police investigator was being sent from the capital. I should install myself in his body, for he was bound to die.

—*You're going to enter the policeman. Leave the rest to me.*

—*How long am I going to be out there in life?*

—*Six days. That's how long it'll take for the policeman to die.*

This was the first time I was going to leave death. For the very first time I would be able to listen to human voices in the refuge, free of the earth's filter. To hear the old folk without them being aware of me. But then I was furrowed by a doubt. Suppose at the end of it, I enjoyed being a night spirit? And what if, upon dying for a second time, I had fallen in love with the other side? After all, I was lonely in my death. I had never been anything but a pre-ancestor. What surprised me was that I had almost no recollection of the time when I was alive. I could only remember one or two moments, but always things outside myself. In particular, I could remember the smell of the

earth when it rained. Watching the rain flow through
January, I would ask myself: how do we know this smell is
of the earth rather than the sky? On the other hand, I
couldn't recall any intimate detail of the life I had led. Is
that always the case? Do all the dead lose their private
memories? I don't know. In my case, though, I had set my
sights on gaining access to my private experiences. What I
really and truly yearned to remember were the women I
had loved. I confessed my desire to the anteater.

—*As soon as you reach life, burn some pumpkin seeds*, he
suggested.

—*What for?*

—*Don't you know? Burning seeds brings back the memory of
forgotten loves.*

But the next day, I reconsidered my journey into life.
That anteater of mine was already more dead than alive.
Could I really have any confidence in his powers? His
body creaked like a bend in the road. He was exhausted
because of the weight of his shell. The scaly anteater is like
a tortoise – it carries its home along with it on its travels.
That's why it is always so tired.

I called the *halakavuma* and told him I had decided not
to cross over into life. He must understand: a crocodile's
strength is water. My strength was to be far away from the
living. I had never known how to live, even when I was
alive. Now, if I plunged into another man's flesh, I would
be chewed by my own nails.

—*Look here, Ermelindo: go, the weather there is beautiful,
and moistened with good rains.*

I should go, and wrap my soul in green. Who knows,

I might find a woman and stumble into love? The anteater greased his talk and larded his description. He knew it wasn't so easy. I was afraid, as afraid as the living feel when they imagine dying. The anteater gave me assurances of a more-than-perfect future. Everything would happen right there on that very same terrace, under the tree where I was buried. I looked at the frangipani and already I began to miss it. The tree and I were alike. Who had ever watered our roots? Both of us were creatures reared on the mist. The *halakavuma* also had his reasons to be grateful to the tree. Pointing at the terrace, he said

—*This is where the gods come to pray.*

2 *First appearance among the living*

This man I am occupying is a certain Izidine Naíta, a
police inspector. His way of life is adjacent to that of dogs:
he sniffs at misdeeds which drip with blood. I'm in one
corner of his mind, I watch him with great care so as not
to disturb his inner workings. For this man, Izidine, is now
me. I go with him, I go in him, I go him. I talk to
whoever he talks to. I desire whoever he desires. I dream
of whoever he dreams.

At this very moment, for example, I am travelling in a
helicopter, sent on a mission in the nation's service. My
host is rummaging around for clues as to who killed
Vastsome Excellency, a mulatto who was responsible for
the old people's refuge at São Nicolau. Izidine is going to
have to negotiate labyrinths and obstacles. With him, I am
migrating into the darkened territory of shadows,
deception and lies.

I peep out from the clouds over the giddy heights.
Down below, facing the ocean, I can see the old colonial
fort. That is where the refuge is, that's where I am buried.
It's funny how I shot up into the clouds from the depths.
I look out of the window. The fort of São Nicolau is a

tiny smudge within a smidgen of world. As for my grave, you can't even make it out. Seen from up here, the fort is anything but a stronghold. You can see its ruins tumbling away down the cliffs like ribs, opposite the rocky beach. That monument whose beauty the colonists sought to make eternal was now crumbling away. The wooden jetty, which I had nailed together, was now all but rotted through, defenceless against time and the salty air.

During the long years of the war, the refuge had been cut off from the rest of the country. The place had severed its links with the world. The rocky beach hindered access from the sea. Inland, minefields completed the siege. São Nicolau could only be reached by air. All supplies and visitors arrived by helicopter.

Recently, peace had been established throughout the country. But in the refuge, not much had changed. The fort was still surrounded by mines and no one dared to leave or enter it. Only one of the inmates, an old woman called Little Miss No, dared to wander into the surrounding bushland. But her body was so lightweight that she would never have set off an explosive. While I had been dead, I had felt this old woman's feet treading on my slumber. And they felt like caresses, the magic touch of a human being.

Now, I was smuggling myself across the frontier that had once separated me from the light. This Izidine Naíta, this man who is carrying me, has only got six days to live. Does he suspect he's near his end? Is that why he's in such a hurry now, determined to gain time? I accompany the man's movements as he opens a briefcase full of typed papers. On the cover, the word *Dossier* is written. I can see a photograph. Izidine points at the picture and asks out loud

—*Was this Vastsome Excellency?*

—*Can I have a closer look?*

I look at our fellow passenger, sitting in the helicopter's rear seat. I think to myself what a pity it is I didn't occupy that body. Marta Gimo was a woman to look at and lick with your eyes. She had been a nurse at the refuge at the time of the crime. She had only gone to Maputo to make her statement as a witness.

—*I don't see any sign of Vastsome's wife here*, said Izidine, his finger wandering over the photo.

Marta didn't react. She looked at the sea far below, as if struck by sudden sad thoughts. With the photo in her hand, she answered with a sigh

—*At the time, his wife hadn't yet come to São Nicolau.*

She sat there lost in her thoughts, the photograph lying on the seat. My attention turned to Izidine and I pitied this man who had become my dwelling place: he was lost, brimming with doubts. What did he know? That a week before, a helicopter had flown to the fort to fetch Vastsome Excellency and his wife, Ernestina. Excellency had been promoted to an important post in the central government. But when they got to São Nicolau, he was already dead. He'd been murdered. No one knew who had done it or why. What was certain was that the helicopter crew had found Excellency's body sprawled across the rocks below the front rampart. They saw it as the helicopter came in to land.

The moment they touched down, they clambered down the slope to recover the body. But, when they got to the rocks, there was no sign of Excellency's remains. They searched the immediate area. In vain. The corpse had vanished without trace. The waves had carried it off, or at least that's what they thought. They gave up the search and, as night was falling, they set out on their journey back. But as they flew over the area, they spotted the body once again, spreadeagled across the boulders. How had it got back there? Was he alive after all? Impossible. They could see he was covered in wounds, and there was no sign of any movement. They circled the spot but there was no question of the chopper being able to land there, and so they returned to the city. That's what had happened.

—*We're arriving!*

Marta was waving at a little group of old folk. The pilot gave us instructions: no sooner had we touched down than we should get out without delay. He had just enough fuel for the return journey. The chopper's blades echoed off the stone walls and clouds of dust swirled upwards. We jumped out, while the old people huddled together like puppies. They held on to their clothes as if they were about to float away. One of them clung to a flagpole with both hands, looking like a flag in a high wind.

When the helicopter had taken off again, they went back to their corners. Marta strolled around, greeting each one. Izidine tried to approach them but the old timers slunk away, shy and untamed. What were they afraid of?

The helicopter became a dot on the horizon and then

vanished, and Izidine Naíta began to feel vulnerable, lost among beings who shielded themselves from contact. The same helicopter would only return a week later to take him back to the city. The inspector had just seven days to find the murderer. He had no credible sources, no clues. Even the victim's body hadn't survived. That left him witnesses whose memory and lucidity had died away long ago.

He put his bag down on a stone seat. He surveyed the surroundings and wandered off along the ramparts. The sun would soon go down. One or two bats were launching themselves in blind flutterings from the eaves. The elderly inmates were making for the darkness of their rooms. The inspector didn't linger, for fear that the fading light would disappear completely. When he got back, he found an old man rummaging through his bag. The intruder fled. Izidine quickly checked the contents of his bag. He breathed a sigh of relief: the pistol was still there.

—*Are you looking for a torch?*

The policeman jumped with fright. He hadn't noticed Marta's approach. The nurse pointed to a nearby room and gave him a candle and a box with a few matches in it.

—*Use the candle sparingly, it's the only one.*

The inspector stepped into the room which was already shrouded in darkness. He lit the candle and unpacked his bag. A small tin fell to the floor. He picked it up: it wasn't a tin after all. Was it a piece of wood maybe? It looked more like a piece of a tortoise's scaly shell. Izidine was puzzled: how had that come out of his bag? He turned the shell over between his fingers and then threw it out of the window. Afterwards, he went outside again.

Izidine had a plan: every night, he would interview one of the old timers. During the day, he would pursue his investigations on the ground. After dinner, he would sit down by the fire and listen to each one's story. The next morning, he would write down everything he had heard the previous night. That's how this little notebook came into being, this book full of the inspector's handwriting, recording the words of the elders, and which I now carry to the depths of my grave. The little notebook will rot away along with my remains. The creatures of the soil will feed upon these ancient voices.

The inspector then wondered who to listen to first. But it wasn't him who did the choosing. The first old man appeared as soon as Izidine left his quarters. In the half light he looked like a child. He was carrying a hoop made from a bicycle wheel. He sat down, putting the hoop round his neck. Izidine asked him for his version of what had occurred there. The old man asked

—*Have you got all night's time?*

He put the man at ease: indeed he had all night. The old man grinned impishly. Then he explained

—*It's because we talk too much. And do you know why? Because we're alone. We don't even have God to keep us company. Do you see over there?*

—*There? Where?*

—*Those clouds in the sky. They're like these cataracts in my eyes: mists that prevent God from getting a glimpse of us. That's why we are free to tell lies here in this fort.*

—*Before we talk about the death of the director, I want to know if it was you who went through my bag!*

3 Navaia's confession

Who, me? Go through your things? You can ask anyone: I didn't tamper with your case, or so much as touch it. Someone did it. Not me, Navaia Caetano. I'm not going to say who it was. Mouths talk but don't point. Besides, the bat wept because of its mouth. But I saw the meddler. Indeed I did. It was a shape picking over your things like a vulture, sir. That shadow flew down and perched on my eyes, perched in every corner of the darkness. And it didn't seem to be made in the form of a human being. Believe me, the very memory of it sends a shiver through my soul.

But now let me ask you: was anything taken? It's just that the old folk here are all takers. They don't steal. Just take. They take things without even getting as far as stealing them. Let me explain: here in this fort, no one owns anything. So if there are no owners, there's nothing to steal. Isn't that so? Here, it's the grass that eats the cow.

I deny any theft but I confess to the crime. Let me say this straight away, inspector: I'm the one who killed Vastsome Excellency. You needn't look any further. It was me, yours truly. And I'll tell you something else that's even closer to the truth: that mulatto killed himself using my hands. He was the one who condemned himself, I just executed his murderous desires. If I carried out my actions with body and soul, it was not out of hatred. I haven't the strength to hate. I'm like a worm: I don't harbour grudges against anyone. A worm, inspector, flat and blind as he is, who can he hate?

If your patience allows, I'll explain. Come into the light a bit more. Don't be afraid of the smoke. Don't even fear getting burnt: there's no other way of listening to me. My voice grows weaker and weaker the longer I go on unravelling these confidences. Keep quiet as you listen to these stories. Silence makes the windows through which we glimpse the world. Don't write anything down, and leave that notebook on the ground. Be like water in a glass. He who is a drop always drips, he who is dew evaporates. Here in this refuge, your ears will grow bigger. For we live to talk.

It all began in the time beyond time. We say *ntumbuluku* which means when the first people came into the world. It seems far away, but it's there that the days are born when still in bud. This man, Excellency, began to die before he was born. It began with me, the old man–child.

I, Navaia Caetano, am the victim of a curse that weighs heavily upon me: I suffer the illness of premature age. I'm a little child who grew old the moment he was born. That's why they say I'm forbidden to tell my own story. When I finish my tale, I shall be dead. Or, who knows, maybe not? Can it really be true that I am condemned to suffer such a fate? Even so, I shall begin, and make of my words time's hiding place. As I continue with my tale, I feel older and more weary. Do you see these wrinkles on my arms? They are new, I didn't have them before I started talking to you. But I shall continue, seeking neither relief nor short cut. I'm like a pain without flesh to suffer in, I'm like a nail that persists in growing on a severed foot. Give me the patience of your ears, sir.

My uncle on my mother's side, Taúlo Guiraze, told me this: other people tell their life's story in a light-hearted way. But not an old man–child. While others age just their words, in my case, all of me ages. And so this was my uncle's advice.

—*My boy, I know a solution to your problem. If one day you decide to become a storyteller. . .*

—*And what would that be?*

He had heard talk of an old man–child born elsewhere, elsewhen. This child, seeing the anguish of others at his impending death, amused himself by telling them his history. But when he'd finished all his many tales, he was still alive.

—*He didn't die, and do you know why? Because he lied. His stories were all made up.*

Was my uncle inviting me to lie? Only he could know. What I'm going to tell you now, under peril of death, are disjointed episodes of my life. All in order to explain what happened here at the refuge. I know I'm filling your writing with my saliva. But when I've finished, sir, you'll understand all my warbling.

I'll begin by talking about my mother. I've never

known such a fertile woman. How many times did she jump the moon? She produced many a child. Yes, I mean just that: child, not children. For she would always give birth to the same creature. When she bore a new child, the previous one would disappear. But all the ones who followed were identical, drops feeding the same water. Folk in the village suspected punishment, some failure to obey the old laws. So what was the reason for such punishment? No one spoke out loud, but everyone knew the reason for the curse: my father was always visiting my mother's body. He wasn't patient enough to wait while my mother was producing her milk. That was what tradition required: a woman's body is untouchable during her first milk. My old man disobeyed. He himself boasted he'd found a way round the obstacle. He would take a magic string with him on his love-makings. When he was ready to knead his wife, he would tie a knot round the child's waist. Love could then take place without any consequences.

My mother's tainted fate was thus apparently sealed. I stress the word 'apparently', because my own tragedy began at that point. I know that now: I was born from one of those badly-tied knots around the waist of a dead brother.

Don't worry, inspector, I'm getting to myself. Don't you remember what I said? I was born into a fragile little body, always spared from thirst. My arrival seemed to have been blessed: the six seeds of the *hacata* had been cast. They had fallen well, aligned by good spirits.

—*This child will be more ancient than life itself.*

My grandfather lifted me up to be blessed and held me aloft. He did not speak, as if he were weighing my soul. Who knows what he was seeking? Among the thousands of living creatures, only man listens to silences. Then my grandfather clasped me to his chest, once again full of laughter. But he was deceived in his joy. I lay under a curse. I was made aware of this curse the first few times I cried. As I wept, I began to disappear. My tears washed away my bodily matter, dissolved my substance. But that wasn't the only sign of my condition. Before that, I had been born free of my mother's labour. As I left her body, she suffered no pains, for I was devoid of substance. I slid through her belly, drained from my mother's flesh, more liquid than blood itself.

My mother then had a prediction that I was heaven's gift. She called my father, who lowered his eyes, because a man is forbidden to face his son until the umbilical cord has fallen. My old man sent for the soothsayer, who sniffed my spirits, sneezed, coughed and then gave his prognosis.

—*This child must not suffer any sadness. Any sadness, however slight, will be doubly fatal.*

My old man nodded, pretending he understood. It looks bad for a man to ask another to explain his words. It was my mother who confessed she didn't understand.

—*What I'm saying, mother, is that if the child cries, he may never reappear.*

—*Is one tear enough?*

—*Less than one. The merest fleck of a tear is enough.*

Tears were confirmation of my childhood, denying my

aged body. The soothsayer was once again seized by
convulsions. The spirits were speaking through his mouth
but, before that, it was as if they were crossing the deepest
recesses of my flesh. The soothsayer's powerful voice
continued, now hoarse, now chanting. It poured out its
sentences and increased its pitch in spasms. Sometimes it
was a mere trickle, without any body to it. Other times, it
was a torrent startled by its own grandiloquence.

I was more newly-fledged than fledgling, but I could
already understand everything I heard. The medicine man
asked me something in Ndau, a language I didn't know,
and still don't know. But someone inside me took over
my voice and answered in that strange tongue. When the
soothsayer cast the bones, they told him I should wear a
tsungulo. He put the string of cloth beads round my neck.
I didn't know this, but wrapped inside the cloth were the
remedies against sadness. This charm would defend me
against time.

—*Now, go.*

And he explained: those words were keys that broke
inside the locks once the doors had been opened. They
couldn't be used a second time. My mother fell silent and,
lost in her own thoughts, dragged me homewards.

—*Mother: what illness have I got?*

My mother squeezed me hard. Never again would I
feel such strength in her hand.

—*I can't talk about it, my son.*

She seemed to be on the verge of tears. But no, she just
turned her face away. And she walked off, head bowed. I
inherited this way of growing sad from my mother: only

when I'm not crying do I believe in my tears. At that
moment, only my uncle Taúlo could reveal the cause of
my sufferings to me.

—*You, my little Caetano, you have no age.*

So that's how it was: I had been born, grew up and
reached my dotage all on the same day. A person's life
stretches out over years, like a parcel being slowly
unwrapped, but which never falls into the hands of the
person it's intended for. My life, on the other hand, had
been spent in just one day. In the morning, I was an
infant, kittenishly crawling around on all fours. In the
afternoon, I was a grown man, confident in my step and
my speech. At night, my skin was already growing
wrinkled, my voice fading, and I was pained by regret at
not having lived my life.

The first day passed, and my family summoned the
villagers and asked them to wait outside our house. A
child born in such a way must surely be the bearer of
tidings, warnings about the future of their land. By that
time, my appearance was no longer attractive: my skin had
more wrinkles than a turtle, my hair had grown and my
nails were long and curved like a lizard's. My hunger was
endless and when my poor mother gave me her breast, I
sucked with such eagerness that she almost fainted. She
was preparing to feed me again when my uncle Taúlo
raised his arm and called a halt to the proceedings.

—*Let no woman offer him her breast.*

He had been forewarned. He recalled another old
man–child: he sucked at his mother's breast with such
gusto that she couldn't withstand it and died, withered

like sugarcane that's been put through the press. His aunts came and offered him their breasts: they died too. With his arm still held out, my uncle Taúlo concluded

—*Let no one suckle him!*

My mother swatted an invisible fly and came over to me, taking me onto her lap.

—*I can't allow my son to go hungry,* she said.

And she pulled her breast out from under her *capulana,* the long piece of cloth wrapped round her body. Those present averted their gaze. All refused to watch, even my uncle. It was a pity. For no one witnessed how she died.

That was when they sent me packing, banished me to this refuge. I bore a curse, I was contaminated by a *mupfukwa,* the spirit of those who had died because of me. My illness was to have been born. I'm paying for it with my own life. A further punishment preys on my mind: when I finish telling my story, I shall die. Like those mothers whose babies feed from their breast until they are drained of life. Now I understand. The act of birth is a sham: we are not born as a result of it. We are already being born beforehand. People awaken in a preceding time, prior to being born. It's like a plant that, within the secrecy of the soil is already a root, before proclaiming its greenery in the world above.

What's the matter, inspector? Are you listening to the owl? Don't be afraid. It's my mistress, I belong to that bird. That owl has taken me under her wing and provides for me. Every night, she brings me scraps of food. She scares you, sir. I understand, inspector. The hoot of an owl echoes through the hollowness of our soul. Folk shudder when they actually glimpse the holes through which we drain away. I used to be scared too. But now, her hooting warms my nights. In a moment I'll go and see what she's brought me this time.

I've lost my way, you're saying to yourself. No, I'm just chasing away the mist. When you get round to the business of lining up your suspects, you'll think that it was the old Portuguese, Domingos Mourão, who killed the director. You haven't met him yet? Tomorrow, you'll see him. After talking to that white man, you'll decide one way or the other. But mark my words, inspector: it was I who killed Vastsome Excellency. It's true: the Portuguese will lay before you his reasons for putting the mulatto to death. But mine are more powerful. You'll see. Let me continue pulling together my memories.

When I came to the refuge, I knew this would be my last and final dwelling place. I felt worn out, for days and days I didn't touch a crust. I was so hungry that if I didn't die, it was because death couldn't find me, so skinny had I become. Then I befriended the owl, and was given some scraps from her leftovers. Then, much later, my hopes were raised by some news.

At that time, an old woman called Little Miss No came to the refuge. People began to talk straight away: she was a witch. An idea flashed through my mind: maybe she could help me return to my true age! I spoke to this Miss No. At first the witch refused. She claimed she didn't have the power. My hopes were dashed.

One day, however, she changed her mind without any

explanation. She called me to say she would prepare a
ceremony in order to catch the *mupfukwa*, the evil spirit
who was persecuting me. She needed an animal, for it was
necessary to have blood soak into the ground. But where
was I going to lay my hands on an animal round there? I
spoke to the owl and asked her to bring me a live
creature. That night I got a dying heron. But the bird's
blood was so light that it didn't fall to the floor. I had to
seize it by the neck. We were ready to begin the
ceremony. Little Miss No was unequivocal: my mother's
spirit needed placating.

—*What does she want?* I asked.

My old mother spoke through the witch's voice: peace
would only visit me if, in exchange, I conceded peace to
her. I should give my childhood full rein. During the day,
I should busy myself in play, spinning my merriment
round the old fort. I was to be a complete child, so that
she could listen to my fun and games. And find solace in
her motherly role.

From then on, my cries and laughter lit up the
corridors of the refuge. I was an infant almost all the time.
During the day, my childlike side ruled my body. At night,
old age weighed upon me. Lying in my bed, I would call
the other old folk to come and listen to a bit of my story.
My companions were aware of the mortal danger of those
tales. At the end of an episode, I might be swallowed up
by death. In spite of this, they would ask me to go on
with my narratives. I would unpick tale after tale, and they
would grow tired.

—*Fuck me! The fellow's still not dead . . .*

—*We'll end when the stories end, but he'll still be alive and kicking . . .*

—*He's making it all up, for sure. He's giving truth the slip.*

It was true I was making it up. But not always, not everything. One night, after a lot of prattling, I felt exhausted. I thought: I must be near the end now! Stars I had never seen before on any night passed before my eyes. Words no longer flowed through my mouth. Could it be that I had died?

No, my chest still heaved. And what was stranger still, as I brushed past the very last frontier, my body began to unwrinkle, I was losing my elderly look. Was my life reaching the time for it to end, and was I into blossoming rebirth?

The old folk looked at one another: had I spoken the truth this time? I sensed that some of them were weeping. At first, they had yearned to see death's spectacle. Now, they were repentant. For that which was dying in me did not, after all, bear any resemblance to them. It was a child, a creature immersed in its infancy. That child could not die. Suddenly, they missed my childish pranks. I was the only light to brighten the darkness of those corridors. Who would play with my hoop now? That bicycle wheel that used to race noisily down the corridors, who would now roll it giddily along?

Seeing me die, they reached a decision. They must arrange an immediate, but genuine ceremony. The salvation of that child, me Navaia Caetano, must be guaranteed. And so they prepared things: drums, *capulanas*, special clothes hidden away for such occasions.

Everything to placate the spirit that had lodged in me.

—*Do you mean we had all those things here?*

Yes, they had even invented drums. They improvised with cooking pots and bits of pipe. When it comes to it, sadness can find ways of making music. The previous night they had prepared the fire-water. They pilfered some ingredients from the food store in the refuge. For hours, they made merry, drinking, stuffing their mouths to excess. From time to time, they would look over at me as I lay in my bed: I was still alive. Then they would dance and sing once more. Even the old Portuguese was persuaded to dance. The witch placed both her hands over the white man's face and said

—*I want to know what language your demon speaks.*

That's what Little Miss No said, exhorting everyone to go on dancing. Then they passed smoking herbs from hand to hand, and their incense spread, making them feel dizzy.

—*I can see the ocean*, said the white man.

That didn't surprise her: the old Portuguese could always see the ocean, it was all he could see. The witch then shuffled her arms, gesticulating wildly, and fell into a trance. She looked as if her body were taking leave of her soul. She spoke in another voice which emerged from her depths. I bade the others keep quiet.

—*Let us listen.*

—*The spirit's talking Portuguese.*

—*Is that Portuguese? I can't understand it . . .*

It was Portuguese, but from the old days. The spirit was that of a white soldier who had died in the courtyard of

the fort. This Portuguese, the witch told us, was waiting
for a ship, and looking out to sea.

　—*It's like you, Domingos, always looking at the sea.*

　—*But I'm not waiting for a ship . . .*

　—*That's what you think, old fellow.*

　—*Keep quiet, let us hear the spirit.*

　—*Yes, we want to know who this soldier is.*

The soldier had fallen ill, almost gone mad. From
looking at the sea so much, his eyes had changed colour.
The last thing he saw was the storm coming, like the
white widowhood of the heron. Then, his eyes were gone.
He was left with two sockets, caves into which no one
dared peer. He died without a burial, without a
farewell . . .

Suddenly, there was a rumble. It was as if the war had
returned. We stopped dancing and looked apprehensively
at Little Miss No. She reassured us: it was only two clouds
colliding with each other. I looked at the sky, but there
was no sign of a cloud. Against the star-studded
background of night I could see nothing except for the
fleeting passage of a bird of prey. Proudly, it crossed the
clear night sky. Might it be the owl? And where, then,
were the clouds scraping against each other? Then there
was a second rumble, this time much nearer. I looked:
there he was, the director, kicking over the drum
containing the fire-water. The liquor poured out onto the
ground and was lost. The ancestors had never had so
much to drink.

　—*What's all this shit? What's going on here?*

Our ritual had been rudely interrupted by Vastsome

Excellency. The director mouthed abuse at us, sullying our name.

—*Didn't I tell you this sort of buffoonery was forbidden in the refuge?*

The other old folk explained: the ritual was being performed in order to save me. The mulatto, startled, looked in my direction. He walked over to my bed as if he wanted to satisfy himself about my identity. When his eyes met mine, it was as if they had been struck by a blow. He shook his head and rubbed his eyelids, impeding his vision. Then he turned his back on me and declared

—*Either you clear this filth up immediately, or I'll torch everything, drinks, old folk, children, the lot.*

And he left. The old timers looked at each other, emptier than the fire-water. Little Miss No got up and came over to my bed. She lifted the sheet and began to rub my legs with oils. —*His strength will come back to him,* she said. I felt a warmth spreading through my innermost bones. After a while, the witch encouraged me to get out of bed.

—*Go on, Navaia. Do what you've got to do . . .*

I got up without effort. It was as if an invisible hand were pushing me. And voices urged me on.

—*You're a true child, you've got a child's strength.*

—*Yes, Navaia, go and kill that sonofabitch . . .*

I closed my eyes. So had death argued over my body in order for me to kill? I unclenched my hands. Leaning on the old folk, I was led towards the door. The moonlight fell upon me. Only then did I notice a dagger in my right hand, gleaming and upright.

4 Second day among the living

On the second morning, I waited for Izidine to stir again. It would be the second time he had woken that morning. Marta had already made him jump out of bed once. She had brought him a cup of tea. The policeman drank it in one gulp, his eyes wrapped in sleep. What with the rats, cockroaches and nightmares, he didn't have much head left for thought. Marta laughed when she saw him in this state, and left so that he might rest a little more. The policeman had gone straight back to sleep. How he had slept that night! Did he suspect my presence inside him? It's very unlikely: I weigh less than the mist on a cobweb.

Izidine woke up again some hours later. Before getting out of bed, he looked at his clothes lying in a mess on an old table. Had he really left them scattered about like that? Suddenly, next to his hat, he saw the scaly piece of shell he had thrown away the previous night. He got out of bed and picked it up. He put it in a jacket pocket. Then, he embarked on a plan he had drawn up earlier: he went down to the beach to clamber over the great rocks, right down where the surf pounded. It was there that the body had been found.

The tide was out and had left stretches of sand and rock uncovered. The gulls could be heard, screeching in a melancholy way. Before long, one would be able to hear the plovers, those white-fronted little birds that summon in the tide. The tide rises and falls in obedience to those birds. Just a short while ago, it was the sandpipers that had ordered the waters to ebb. Curious how such a gigantic creature as the ocean is so attentive to the commands of such insignificant little birds.

In days gone by, there had been an anchorage next to the rocky reef. I myself, Ermelindo Mucanga, had begun to carpenter the jetty. Death had interrupted my work. Independence put an end to the rest of the project. Then, the sea had taken its revenge on the unfinished harbour. All that was left were some loose stones, a rotting jetty and some tree trunks that obstinately clung to the waves down there.

Izidine sat down on the damp sand. The noise of the surf helped him to think. It was obvious that the crime had been committed by more than one person. It would have taken more than one man to carry a body like that of Vastsome Excellency. Or, who knows, maybe the crime was committed right there, next to the rocks?

He cast his gaze towards the rampart and saw Marta. She was looking at him surreptitiously, following his movements. The nurse behaved as if she suspected him of some secret intentions. That morning, after handing the inspector his tea, she had refused to accompany him.

—*I don't want to get in your way. It's enough to have you getting in your own way . . .*

—*I'm sorry, but I don't understand . . .*

Marta fell silent, sorry she had spoken. She ignored his request for an explanation. Finally, she agreed to talk, pretending to flick a speck of dust from his shirt.

—*What we discover in this life does not come as the result of our searching for it.*

Her advice to the policeman was quite simply that he should sit and wait quietly. This was not his world, he had to respect it. He should leave everything as it was, including silences and absences. Izidine bore witness to his doubts. The previous night, the old man–child had already thrown enough dust in his eyes. Navaia Caetano had asked him to listen to the sea. For, as well as the roar of the sea, he would also hear human cries.

—*Cries?* asked Izidine. —*Whose cries?*

—*The cries of the dead,* Caetano had replied.

And he said no more. The inspector's curiosity was aroused. Why was it that Marta Gimo was now all but asking the opposite of him?

—*Yesterday, I was asked to listen. You are asking the opposite.*

—*What did they ask you to listen to?*

He repeated Navaia's enigmatic advice. What did he mean? Surely Marta could help clarify this. But she smiled and shook her head. The nurse was being awkward. Izidine asked her again. Finally, she gave in. What the old man had said was that under the crash of the surf lay hidden the voices of shipwrecked mariners, drowned fishermen, and women who had killed themselves. Among these lamentations, he was bound to hear the cries of Vastsome Excellency himself. The policeman smiled scornfully. Marta corrected him in his scepticism.

—*Don't you realise how arrogant you are? Well, you may be sure that every morning the dead man shouts out his assassin's name.*

—*I can't believe it.*

—*Every morning, the dead man swears vengeance.*

Now, sitting close to where the surf thunders onto the beach, the inspector recalled the nurse's words. And he smiled. Could it be that Marta was right? He had studied in Europe, had returned to Mozambique some years after independence. Separation had curtailed his knowledge of the culture, of the languages, of the little things that shape a people's soul. Back in Mozambique he had gone straight into an office job in the capital. His day-to-day experience was limited to a tiny corner of Maputo. Little more than that. In the countryside, he was no more than an outsider.

He got to his feet and shook the sand off himself. There was a certain anger in his gesture, as if he not only wanted to brush away the grains of sand, but his memories as well. He wandered across the rocks. Until he came across a rifle. It wasn't hidden. It looked as if it had been washed in by the waves. He searched the immediate vicinity. There were some splinters of wood. They looked like pieces of a raft. Had there been a vessel there, even though everyone had told him that those waters were so dangerous? He recalled old Navaia's words.

—*The sea here contains more treachery than it does waves.*

The previous night, Navaia had told him a story. It had

happened a long time ago, when an old man had tried to escape by sea. He had built a makeshift raft and set off. But the rocks and the sea, as if by magic, swapped appearances. That which the fugitive took for waves suddenly turned to stone. And the great boulders dissolved into liquid. His boat broke up. The old man's dreams of escape remained unfulfilled.

Was Navaia drawing this story from his imagination? Whether or not the tale was an invention, what was certain was that those waters didn't counsel a journey. Was the story of the raft true after all? Was this a tangible relic of his frustrated flight? Suspicion furrowed the inspector's brow: they were hiding something from him. In his distraction, he didn't even notice that night was falling. He set off back to the fort at a brisk pace. That night he had arranged to meet the old Portuguese, Domingos Mourão. He waited for him in the courtyard, but the other was late. The policeman sat on the outer parapet of the fort, and was conscious of the roar of the ocean down below. Suddenly, he was sure he could hear the sound of real voices coming from the beach.

—*It's not people making that noise.*

It turned out to be Marta emerging from the darkness, wrapped in a *capulana*. She came up and stopped next to him. They stood there, silent sentinels of the fort.

—*Could it be the sea making that noise?*

—*No, it's not the sea either. That noise is night itself. People long ago stopped listening to the night where you come from.*

Then she sat down, covering her legs with her *capulana*. She began to sing a traditional lullaby in a low voice.

Izidine was transported far away, far from the present and its possible events.

—*My mother used to sing me that same tune.*

But Marta was no longer there. She had withdrawn, a wandering shadow. The policeman continued to sit there, trying to decipher the sounds that came from the shoreline. His eyelids began to grow heavy and he was eventually overcome by sleep. He awoke a few moments later. The touch of a hand brought him back to reality. It was the old Portuguese.

—*Come and watch the sea from up here!*

Domingos Mourão settled himself on a stone seat next to the frangipani tree. And, his eyes fixed on the horizon, he asked him

—*Begging your pardon for my bluntness, but were you born by the sea?*

Izidine shook his head. The Portuguese said that he had heard of a far-off land where, when night fell, the old folk sat down on the beach. There they remained in silence. The sea would come in and choose the one to be taken away.

—*Who knows whether, this very night, I may be the chosen one?*

And the old Portuguese closed his eyes, absorbed inside his lengthy silence. Then he spoke.

5 The confession of the old Portuguese

—How the ocean lives at ease with itself here!

That's what I said that afternoon. Was I speaking to no one? No, I was talking to the waves down there. I'm Portuguese, Domingos Mourão my name from birth. Here, they call me Sidimingo, and I grew to like it: such a name saves me the trouble of having to remember myself. Inspector, you are asking for easily remembered recollections. If you want to know, I'll tell you. It all happened here on the terrace, under this frangipani tree.

My life was engulfed by the perfume of its white flowers, with their yellow heart. Now there is no smell, for it is not the flowering season. Inspector, you are black. You can't understand why I have always loved these trees, It's because here, in your country, there are no other trees that shed their leaves. Only this one becomes bare, as if winter were approaching. When I came to Africa, I didn't experience autumn anymore. It was as if time no longer moved forward, as if we were always in the same season. Only the frangipani restored that sense of time passing to me. Not that I need to feel the passage of the days any longer. But the fragrance on this terrace soothes my yearning for the life I used to lead in Mozambique. And what a life it was!

When Independence came, twenty years ago now, my wife left. She went back to Portugal. And she took my little boy, who was at the age when he was beginning to toddle. When she took her leave, she still carped at me

—*If you stay, I never want to see you again.*

I felt as if I had just walked into a marsh. My will was sluggish, my desires wallowing in mud. Yes, I could leave Mozambique. But I could never leave to make a new life. What am I then? A mere shred of nothingness?

Let me tell you a story. It's from the old days, from the time of Vasco da Gama, so I was told. They say that in those days there was an old black man who wandered along the beaches picking up flotsam and jetsam. He collected the remains of shipwrecks and buried them. It so happened that one of the wooden planks he stuck in the ground grew roots and came back to life as a tree.

Well now, mister inspector, I'm that tree. I come from a plank in another world but my ground is here, my roots were reborn in this place. It's these black men here who scatter my seeds every day. Am I tiring you with my talk, with my babble? I'm getting near, like the beetle who circles his hole twice before scuttling down it. Forgive me for my Portuguese, I don't know what language I talk any more, my grammar is all muddy, the colour of this soil. And it's not just my talk that's changed. It's my thinking too, inspector. Even Old Gaffer is sad at the way I've become de-portugoosed. I remember one day he said to me

—*You, Sidimingo, belong to Mozambique, this country is yours. Without a shadow of doubt. But doesn't it make you shiver to think of being buried here?*

—*Here, where?*

—*In a cemetery here, a Mozambican one.*

I shrugged my shoulders. There in the refuge, I wouldn't even be graced with burial in a cemetery. But Old Gaffer was insistent.

—*It's that your spirits don't belong to this place. If you're buried here, you won't have a peaceful death.*

Buried or alive, the truth is I have no peace anyway. You're going to hear a lot round here concerning this old Portuguese, my good sir. They'll tell you what I did and what I caused to happen. That I even burnt the grass that stretches way back over there. And there's some truth in it: I did indeed set fire to that bushland over there. But it was for my own reasons, and at my own command. Every time I looked to the rear of the fort, I saw grassy plains stretching away as far as the eye could see and beyond. Faced with such devastating vastness, I felt an instinctive urge for fire and ash.

Now I know: Africa robs us of our identity. But at the same time as it empties us, it fills our being. That's why, even today, I feel like setting fire to those plains. So that they may lose their eternity. So that they may leave me alone. It's because I'm so rootless, so exiled, that I no longer feel far from anywhere, nor isolated from anyone. I gave myself up to this country like someone converted to a religion. Now I want nothing except to be a stone in this ground. But not just any stone, one of those that never gets trodden on by anybody. I want to be a roadside stone.

I'm getting back to my story, don't worry. Where was I? Seeing off my former wife. That's right. After she had gone, the troubles came, confusion. I tell you this with sadness: the Mozambique I loved is dying. It'll never come back. All that's left is this little patch of ground where I seek the shade of the sea. My nation is this terrace here, this balcony over the ocean.

All these years, I've spread out across this tiny fatherland like an estuary: I flow sleepily, at odds with nothing as I meander along. Here in this shade, I created my own kingdom, enraptured by that gentle murmur, as if it were a lullaby sung at my birth. Only my tired legs occasionally troubled me. But my eyes darted across the horizon like swallows, and made up for the aches and pains of old age.

You know something, my dear inspector, in Portugal there's a lot of sea but not so much ocean. And I love the sea so much that I even like getting seasick. What do I do? I knock back a few drinks, the ones they traditionally make here in these parts, and allow myself to get sozzled. In this dizzy state, I fancy myself on the high seas, adrift in a boat. The same motives draw me over there under the frangipani on the terrace: I fill myself with infinity, and get drunk on it. Yes, I know the dangers involved: he who confuses sky and water ends up unable to distinguish between life and death.

Do I talk a lot about the sea? Let me explain, sir: I'm like a salmon. I live in the sea but I'm always on my way back to where I came from, swimming against the current, jumping waterfalls. I return to the river where I was born to leave my sperm, and then I die. On the other hand, I'm a fish that's lost its memory. While I swim upstream, I gradually invent myself another source. That's when I yearn so strongly for the sea. As if the sea were a womb, the only womb still capable of casting me out into life again.

I'm surpassing myself with verbiage. I'm sorry, I'm no longer used to being with people who have urgent matters and tasks to attend to. Here, no one has any practical purpose whatsoever. What is there to do? I tell my friend, Old Gaffer: it's still too early for us to do anything, so we're waiting for it to be too late. I was always the only white man in this refuge. The others are elderly Mozambicans. All of them black. But the only task any of us have is to wait. What for? You should join us here in these leisurely climes, sir. Don't worry, let your watch rest in peace. From now on, I'll get straight to the point: I'll start again where I left off, on this very terrace where we are now.

Well, it happened one afternoon, when all this blue seemed to be signalling my end: the last gull, the last cloud, the last gasp.

—*Now, indeed, the only thing left for me to do is to die.*

Such were my thoughts, for here folk wither away, dying so slowly that we are not even aware of it. What is old age if not death installing itself in our bodies in gradual stages? Beneath the sweet scent of the frangipani, I envied the sea because, in its very infinity, it aspired to fulfil itself in other waters. I was unravelling such talk to myself, alone. When one is old, one can talk at any hour of the day. I asked God out loud to pluck me from life there and then.

—*God: I want to die today.*

Those selfsame words still send a shiver down me. It's that I felt quietly happy, untroubled by any pain. But at the same time, I lacked the ability to die. My breast obeyed the heaving of the waves, as if it possessed the memory of a time beyond time, there where the wind unfurls its huge tail. Lucky are those of my friends who believe that every day is the third day, suitable for resurrections.

But I was requesting death that afternoon when there were no clouds and the sky had been abandoned by the gulls. It wasn't just the sea that brought about my desire for infinity. It was the frangipani flowers. As if I had become one of the earth's family. As if I were the one in flower.

—*It's true, death wouldn't hurt me today.*

—*I might yet carry out your wish.*

Those words didn't come from me. Nor did I see Vastsome Excellency approaching, the true sonofabitch. Excellency was a mulatto, tall and upright, always well turned out. The fellow laughed, his shoulders shaking.

—*Do you really want to die, old timer? Or isn't it the case that you're already dead and just haven't been told?*

Those words wounded me, as if they'd come from an animal's gullet. The mulatto continued, still making me feel a fool.

—*Don't be afraid, you old grouch. I'm off out of here tomorrow.*

I was surprised, taken aback: the scoundrel was leaving us just like that? And how did he come to be leaving?

—*Don't you believe me?*

I shook my head in denial. Vastsome circled the trunk of the frangipani like a matador studying a bull's neck. He took pleasure in hurting me.

—*And d'you know something else, oldie? I'm going to take my wife with me. Hey, I'm carrying off Ernestina. Do you hear me, oldie? Are you going to say nothing?*

—*What nothing?*

—*Without Ernestina, who are you going to spy on? Mm? What's going to happen, oldie?*

I bit my tongue. Vastsome was inviting me to lose my temper, to answer back. All I could do was back off. Until he jumped up and seized me by the wrists.

—*Do you want to know why I've always treated you badly, Mourão? You, an angel fallen from the Portuguese heavens?*

I pretended to focus on the sky, just so as to avoid his face. I remembered all the countless punishments suffered during those years. The director stamped on my ankles with both feet.

—*It hurts? How can that be? Angels don't have feet!*

And so by treading on my body where it hurt the most, the mulatto, more than anything, was trampling on my spirit.

—*Are you pretending to be a stone? Well, then: aren't stones for treading on?*

I put up with it all, without batting an eyelid. His devil's breath splattered me. A chorus line of insults danced out of his mouth. He pulled my ears and spat in

my face. He got off me and walked away. Then I gave vent
to my pent-up fury: I grabbed a stone and aimed it at the
bastard's head. An unexpected hand stopped me.

—*Don't do that, Sidimingo.*

It was Ernestina, Excellency's wife. She pulled me
towards the stone seat. Her hands cupped my back.

—*Sit down here.*

I obeyed. Ernestina passed her fingers through my hair.
I breathed in the air around me: no smell reached me
from her. Had I been inventing her fragrances?

—*You don't understand his wickedness, do you?*

—*No.*

—*It's because you're white. He has to mistreat you.*

—*Why?*

—*He's scared he'll be called a racist.*

To be honest, I didn't understand. On the other hand,
sitting next to her like that, I didn't need to understand.
The only thing I did was to get up and pick a couple of
flowers. Fragile, their petals loosened as I offered them to
her. Ernestina raised her hands to her face.

—*Good Lord, how I love their scent.*

I smoothed down my Sunday suit. I was no longer
aware of the days or weeks. As far as I was concerned,
every day had the taste of Sunday. Maybe I wanted
whatever time I had left to pass quickly. Ernestina asked
me

—*Don't you feel a longing?*

—*Me?*

—*When you look at the sea like that, don't you feel a
longing?*

I shook my head. Longing? Who for? On the contrary, I enjoy being alone. I swear it, inspector. I enjoy being far away from my people. Not being touched by their complaints, their ailments. Not seeing them grow old. And more than anything, not seeing any of my folk die. Here, I'm far removed from death. It's a tiny morsel of pleasure I still have. The advantage of being far away, separated by such a distance as this, is that one has no family. Family and old friends are there, at the other end of all this sea. Those who die, disappear so far away, they're like shooting stars. They fall noiselessly, without us knowing where or when.

I mean this seriously, inspector: you'll never find out the truth about the dead man. Firstly, these black friends of mine will never tell you what really happened. For them, you're a *mezungo*, a white man like myself. And for centuries, they've learned not to confide in a white man. That's what they've been taught: if you open your heart to a white man, you'll lose your soul, robbed of your innermost self. I know what you're going to say. You're a black man like them. But ask them what they see in you. As far as they are concerned, you're a white, an outsider, someone who doesn't merit their confidences. Being white has nothing to do with race. You know that, don't you? And then there's something else. It's to do with the very rules that govern life. I don't believe in life any more, inspector. Things only pretend to happen. Did Excellency die? Or did he just change his form and become invisible?

I'm going to finish now, inspector. I murdered the director of this refuge. Was it out of jealousy? I don't know. I don't think we ever know the reason when we kill someone out of passion. But now that time has cooled, I can explain things: that afternoon, as I said goodbye to Ernestina, I noticed she was hiding one side of her face. Eventually, I realised what it was. Her face was marked, reddened by a blow.

—*Has Vastsome hit you again?*

She turned her face away. Her hand gripped my arm, urging me to keep quiet. —*Let it be, it's not important,* she said. And she left, her head bowed in the shadow of her shoulders. The woman I loved so much wasn't just one person. She was all the women, all the men who had been defeated by life. At that point, it all seemed straightforward to me: Vastsome ought to be eliminated, I should kill him as soon as possible. Quite simply, I waited for nightfall. At that hour, he always passed down a narrow corridor, without a roof, which linked his room to the kitchen. I set a trap for him up above. I brought a large stone and left it up on top, ready to fall on Vastsome Excellency.

And now, leave me alone, inspector. I find it hard to summon up recollections. For memories reach me torn, in tattered and scattered remnants. I want the peace of belonging to only one place, I want the tranquillity of not having to divide my memories. I want to belong solely to one life. For only then will I be sure to die only once. I find it hard to die so many small deaths, the type we barely notice, deep down in the dark recesses of our inner selves. Leave me, inspector, for I've just died a little bit.

6   Third day among the living

It was my third day back at the fort. Izidine was engulfed by uncertainty. The old people's statements were sending him off along seemingly false trails, but ones which couldn't be ignored. Those elderly folk were vital witnesses, but it was Marta Gimo whom he thought must have the juiciest titbits of information to offer. However, the nurse proved subtly resistant. She shied away from meetings, saying she had work to do. But from what he could see, her time wasn't taken up with nursing. She spent hours joking with the old people, laughing and chatting. She spoke a number of languages and the policeman had no idea what they were talking about. But of one thing he was sure: it was him that Marta and the old timers were laughing at and mocking.

That afternoon, the policeman approached Marta. She was sitting next to Navaia. On this occasion, she did in fact seem to be engaged in her professional duties.

—*Sit down. I'm attending to Navaia.*

The old man–child had rolled up his trousers showing his skinny legs. Marta explained there had been instances of leprosy in the refuge. She was checking to see if this was a new case. Navaia Caetano remarked on the thinness of his legs.

—*It's time, missis nurse. Time is like smoke, for it gradually dries out our flesh.*

Marta Gimo smiled patiently. She got even closer to the old man and uncovered his back in her search for some sign of the illness. Navaia seemed ill at ease.

—*Don't smell me, nurse.*

—*And why not?*

—*Because I smell of snuffed-out candles, the breath of something that's died.*

With one of his hands he stopped the nurse so that he could inspect his legs himself. He seized something and squeezed it between finger and thumb.

—*Do you see this flea, nurse?*

—*I can't see anything.*

—*This flea isn't mine. It's not mine, I know my fleas.*

The nurse smiled and told him to straighten his trousers.

—*What have you been eating, Navaia?*

—*Scraps, the sort of thing they leave lying around for me.*

—*Don't give me the story of the owl, Navaia. That's a tale for the inspector, not for me.*

Then Marta gave him a pat on the back.

—*Right, off you go then. Now I've got to speak to the inspector.*

Navaia crept slowly away; curiosity held him back. He turned round twice pretending to look for his hoop. Finally, when they were alone, Marta held out her hand to the policeman.

—*Before I forget! I was asked to give you this.*

She placed a small object in the palm of his right hand. It was a scale, just like the ones that had appeared in his room.

—*Who gave you this, nurse?*

—*I've forgotten, inspector.*

She spoke with an ironic smile. She pronounced the word *inspector* slowly and deliberately, as if it were an insult. Izidine ignored her sarcastic tone, and came straight to the point.

—*I found a shotgun yesterday, next to the rocks.*

—*A shotgun? That's not possible. You must have made some mistake . . .*

The inspector lost his temper. He berated the nurse: she was totally unwilling to help. She was hiding something. And that was a punishable offence.

—*Listen, inspector, sir: the crime that's been committed here isn't the one you're trying to solve.*

—*What do you mean by that?*

—*Look at these old folk, inspector. They're all dying.*

—*That's what happens to all of us in the end.*

—*But not like this, do you understand? These old folk are not just people.*

—*What are they then?*

—*They are the guardians of a world. It's that world which is slowly being killed off.*

—*I'm sorry, but as far as I'm concerned, that's philosophy. I'm only a policeman.*

—*The real crime being committed here is that they are killing the world of the past . . .*

—*I still don't understand.*

—*They are killing the last surviving roots that might have prevented us from becoming like you . . .*

—*Like me?*

—*Yes, inspector. People without history, people who live by imitation.*

—*This is just idle talk. The truth is that times are changing, these old codgers belong to a past generation.*

—*But these old folk are dying within us.*

And striking her breast, the nurse emphasised the point.

—*It's inside here that they are dying.*

Marta Gimo got up and turned away. Izidine regretted having argued with the woman. Marta was a source of information to be tapped. It would be unwise to alienate her because of a disagreement. He only had three days left. He couldn't waste time. Much less could he cut his links with the person who, it was becoming ever more apparent, was his only lead in solving the mystery of Excellency's death.

That night, just as he was getting ready to go to sleep, he heard a woman's screams. He rushed down the narrow corridors of night. The screams were coming from Marta's room. It was she who was screaming. The policeman burst into her room, pistol in hand. It was dark, and impossible to make out who the nurse was struggling with. Izidine went over and helped shield her from her invisible assailant. Marta fell over while the policeman tried in vain to lay his hands on the intruder. Suddenly, Marta Gimo burst out laughing. Bent double, and gasping for breath because of her laughter, she opened the door and went out into the moonlight. The contours of her body could be seen under her undergarment.

—*But who was it?* asked Izidine.

—*It was a bat!*

She spoke, her voice mingling with her roars of laughter. Izidine Naíta couldn't even muster up the strength to smile. He contemplated himself, as if in a mirror: a gunman in his underpants. Marta went over to him and passed her hand over his hair.

—*You see? We're covered in bat's hairs.*

Throwing her head back, she laughed. She asked him to put his weapon down.

—*Do you know what we should do now?*

—*What should we do?*

—*Yes, if we were to follow tradition, do you know what we should do?*

—*I've no idea. Maybe we would have a bath?*

—*We should make love.*

Without knowing what to say, the policeman smiled. In his awkwardness, he hurried to leave. But he heard the nurse's last words behind him.

—*What a pity you're not a follower of tradition. What a pity, don't you agree?*

Did you speak to the old Portuguese? I'll wager he told
you about that time he was sitting under the frangipani.
Well, I remember that afternoon very clearly. I arrived on
the terrace and saw the old white man asleep. I breathed a
sigh of relief: what I was about to do required a lot of
shadow and few prying eyes. I came up on tiptoe, raised
my cutlass and delivered the first blow. The blade struck
deep into the soft trunk. I never thought the white man
would wake up. I was wrong. Sidimingo came to with a
start, thrusting out his arms.

—*What in heaven's name are you doing?*

—*Can't you see? I'm cutting down this tree.*

—*Stop it, Old Gaffer, you worthless wretch, that tree's mine.*

—*Yours? Be off with you, whitey, and don't bother me.*

We had never traded words like this before. Domingos
Mourão, Sidimingo to us, got to his feet and stumbling,
launched himself against me. We fought, welded together
in our violence. The white man jostled me, it was as if his
mind had turned into that of a wild animal. But soon our
struggle grew more ragged, as our kicks and blows lost
their vigour. Only the heaving of our tired chests made a

show of strength. We shook each other aggressively.

—*You're always trying to order me about. Colonialism's over, you know!*

—*I don't want to order anyone about . . .*

—*What do you mean, you don't want to? I don't trust whites. A white is like a chameleon, it never unfurls its tail completely . . .*

—*And you blacks, you find fault with whites, but all you want is to be like them . . .*

—*Whites are like chilli pepper: you know you've eaten it because you can feel your throat burning.*

—*The difference between you and me is that my hair sticks to the comb while combs stick in your hair.*

—*Shut your mouth, Sidimingo. You're nothing but a bag of farts.*

The old white man laughed to himself. Then he set about tidying himself up. His throat hurt, he felt like a giraffe with a crick in its neck. He sat for some time without moving, his eyes half-closed. He seemed to have passed out.

—*Are you breathing, Mourão?*

—*Listen, Old Gaffer: do you want me to hit you again?*

—*You're the one who got the hiding, whitey . . .*

—*Let me rest a bit and I'll punch you good and hard.*

—*To punch me, you'll need to take a rest for the next century . . .*

We glanced at each other in all seriousness. Then, suddenly, we burst out laughing. We joined fists and slapped palms in agreement. We'd been fighting over a locust, a creature with neither flesh nor sustenance. Then I said to him

—*Sidimingo, my friend, I'm more than a little grateful to you.*

—*Why?*

—*I would have met my maker without ever having hit a white man.*

—*You call that hitting? All I felt was a brush of your fingers . . .*

—*Nonsense. I knocked you around good and proper.*

—*Gaffer, tell me something, you old ratbag: why did you want to cut that tree down?*

I placed the knife under the bench. Then I explained things: all I was trying to do was help Little Miss No. The poor woman had already gathered all the *nkakana* herbs around the fort.

—*But why did she want so much* nkakana?

—*To produce milk, and bring her breasts back to life.*

—*Milk? The old woman is over ninety.*

We talked about Little Miss No, who breastfed imaginary babies, children abandoned during the war. They were her grandchildren, she said. The old woman had become the subject of gossip. Folk said she'd killed her husband so as to keep her children, and had killed her children in order to keep her grandchildren. That's what folk said, and still say. I don't know. What I do know is that after the deaths, Little Miss No had been accused of witchcraft and banished from her home.

—*The old woman is crazy, Gaffer.*

—*I don't know, boss, I really don't know. I'm not sure about anything in this world any more. I sometimes even ask myself which is born first: the horn or the ox?*

The old white man bent down to pick up a flower that had fallen from the tree. The frangipani flowers were food

for the old Portuguese fellow's eyes: he watched them fall
like scales from the sun, white pearls of sweat from the
clouds.

—*I'm going to die very soon, Gaffer. For me, the sky begins
just above those leaves. I can almost touch it . . .*

Such words gave me the shivers. That white man had
been a close companion of mine over recent years and I
couldn't imagine life without him around.

—*Nonsense, boss. We'll sit out on this terrace for many a day
to come.*

—*I'm an old man, my brother. So old, I've even forgotten how
to feel pain.*

His eyes filled with the scent of flowers. He stretched
out his arm and touched the frangipani, as if he wished to
create a whole forest, a kingdom full of shadows and
twittering birds from that one single tree.

—*You touch it too, Gaffer, see how it makes you feel better.*

At that moment, I looked down at my hands and got a
fright.

—*Hey, Mourão, look: my nails have been stolen!*

—*Show me. It's obvious, your claws fell off after the hiding I
gave you . . .*

—*No, can't you see? They've been cut with a blade. It's Miss
No's doing, the old shrew wants to put a spell on me using my nails!*

The incident nearly made me cry with fear. But then
the old Portuguese told me something I'll never forget.

—*Don't be scared, I'm a wizard myself.*

—*A wizard!*

—*I know white man's wizardry. Relax, no one's going to
harm you.*

But it wasn't just fear that gripped me. I was so sad, my eyes became inflamed.

—*Those were my last nails. I shan't live long enough for new ones to grow.*

—*Come now, Gaffer, you're going to live through many a nail. I know when someone is going to die: that's when he wakes up with his navel in the middle of his back.*

—*Don't make me laugh.*

—*It's true: we are born with our navel in our belly, and we die with it the other way round. For example, my uncle woke up with his belly front to back. The same day, he was gone.*

—*Boss, you make me laugh so much. You're a good egg.*

—*That's where you're wrong, Gaffer: I'm not good. I'm just a bit slow in my wickedness.*

The old white man moved off and sat huddled in his own corner. He was waggling his fingers, absorbed in counting them. Why was he counting the fingers on each hand over and over again? Was he scared that he too might have lost his nails?

—*I'm counting my fingers to see if there are any missing . . .*

He feared leprosy, which was common in the area. I chuckled, once again in a joking mood.

—*Hey, Mourão, can't you see? We were fighting!*

—*I enjoyed myself. I punched you full in the face.*

—*It was like Frelimo against fucking colonialism.*

—*We whites always won. For five hundred years we came out on top. We were the ones with the arms . . .*

The Portuguese, poor fellow, stuck to his illusions. He didn't understand the past. We weren't beaten by force of arms. What happened was that we Mozambicans believed the spirits of the new arrivals to be more ancient than our own. We believed that the spells of the Portuguese were stronger. That's why we let them govern us. Who knows, maybe we found their stories more enchanting? Even I, right here in the present, like to listen to the old Portuguese man's stories. Once again, I asked him to entertain me with his fantasies.

—*I'm tired, Gaffer.*

Things tired him that lacked a soul, that was it. At least the tree, he said, had an immortal soul: the earth itself. When you touch its trunk you feel the earth's blood flowing round every vein in your body. And he sat stock still, his eyelids drooping.

—*Are you breathing, Mourão?*

—*Yes, Gaffer. Keep quiet now, so as to listen to the sea . . .*

We sat watching the sea in its deceptive tranquillity. The sky was dotted with the first stars.

—*But why do you attach such importance to that tree?*

—*Just let me talk to the sea.*

I turned and sat down next to the Portuguese. I felt so sorry for him at that moment. The fellow was going to die here, far from his ancestors. He would be buried in a foreign land. In truth, he had been condemned to the most terrible of solitudes: to be far from his own dead, whilst having no one of his own blood to look after him on this side of life. Our gods are near and all around us. His god is far away, out of his sight and out of his plight.

—*Do you pray to God, Sidimingo?*

He shook his head. He only prayed when he didn't want to engage God in conversation, he answered. I chuckled, so as to compensate for the gravity of his offence.

—*You know, Gaffer: I've garnered many a disillusion where God is concerned.*

—*How so?*

—*Here's an example: do you realise how lazy God is?*

—*That's a lie. God holds up the stars, millions of them over millions of nights. Has he ever got tired?*

—*I'm telling you, the fellow's idle.*

—*And why do you say that?*

—*Because he doesn't do any work: he only performs miracles.*

—*Take that back, brother. What you're saying is a crime, a mortal sin.*

—*God doesn't even care about our sins. Do you know the only thing God's interested in? Do you know what it is? He wants to escape from Paradise. Break out of that refuge of his.*

—*Well, in that case, we're like God.*

Suddenly, the white man tired of our banter. He declared that we were wasting our saliva, when the real issue was my mistreatment of his frangipani. He said we blacks couldn't understand because we didn't like trees. At that point, I got angry: what do you mean, we don't like trees? We respect them like members of the family.

—*You whites, you're the ones who don't know what you're talking about. Well, I'm going to teach you something you didn't know.*

So I told him about the origins of time beyond time. In the beginning, the world only contained men. There were no trees, no animals, no stones. Men alone existed. But so many humans were born that the gods realised there were too many and they were all the same. So they decided to turn some men into plants, others into animals. And some, even, into stones. The result? We're all brothers, trees and animals, animals and men, men and stones. We're all related, created out of the same matter.

That's what I told him. But it was as if the Portuguese had heard nothing. He shook his head and said

—*You don't understand, you can't understand. I see you people dreaming of big cars, large houses . . .*

—*And do you dream of small, insignificant things?*

—*My only ambition is to have a tree. Others want forests, but I just want a little tree to tend, to watch it grow and flower.*

—*You talk about Little Miss No and her crankiness. At least her dreams are about filling children's bellies.*

Our talk was exhausting us. We decided to go to sleep then and there, out in the open. We'd had enough of sleeping indoors, listening to old folk snoring, tormented by fleas, rats and cockroaches. We lay down beside each other. We were just drifting off when Mourão shook me.

—*Hey, you, there's no point in trying to park yourself too close.*

Could it be he was confusing my desire for warmth with something else? When I was sure he was already asleep, he spoke again.

—*Gaffer, are you still awake?*

—*I still am, yes. What's wrong, my brother?*

—*It's something I've never had a chance to talk about. It's just that people say we whites have a smaller cock.*

—*I've heard that said too. Show me yours, Sidimingo.*

—*Are you mad? I can't show it to you.* After a short pause, he said —*Well, if you want, you can have a peep.*

The Portuguese raised the elastic of his trousers and drew in his belly.

—*It's true,* I confirmed.

—*What do you mean, it's true?*

—*It's a bit on the tiny side.*

The Portuguese refused to accept my findings. He made a song and dance out of it. I didn't want another argument. And so we soon reached an agreement.

—*Tomorrow morning, early, let's compare them, when they're still awake, doing their overtime.*

We slept the sleep of the elderly, light and fleeting. Every so often I checked the white man's breathing. In the middle of the night, he gave me a sudden fright, pointing his finger at me.

—*Gaffer, you're having a dream, you old rogue . . .*

—*Hey there! Don't you realise you're breaking my sleep, giving me such a jolt?*

—*Serves you right, and it'll teach you not to dream . . .*

—*Come on, Mourão, stop such talk. Now clear up a little doubt I have: can it be that we always dream of women? I always dream of the same woman . . .*

—*Who's that?*

—*It's our Marta. But who told her to undress in front of us, for all the world to see?*

—*The one I like to look at is the boss's wife, that shapely mulatto woman . . .*

—*Ernestina? Be careful there: if Excellency catches you taking a peep, he'll punch your eye out.*

Then we lay down again. We old folk take a while to

get down to the ground. At our age, every movement we make requires a body we no longer have. The white man asked me for a knife, any old piece of blade I might have.

—*What do you want a knife for?*

—*It's so I can dream too.*

Dream? I laughed. Old Mourão believed he only dreamt when he bled. He was adamant. He couldn't dream unless the red stuff was flowing from inside him. That night, there was no way Sidimingo could find peace of mind.

—*Gaffer?*

—*Let me sleep, Sidimingo.*

—*Just one more question: have you ever seen a heron going to sleep?*

—*Yes, why?*

—*It covers its face with its wing. Like a man when he weeps. A heron is ashamed to sleep with the whole world watching. That's what we should do at bedtime.*

At last, he succumbed to sleep. I had been looking forward to that moment. The Portuguese had talked of herons covering themselves with their own wings. My heron was Marta Gimo. She slept naked on the earth, come cold weather, come rain. She covered herself with her arms. It was I who, night after night, saved her from the cold. Marta didn't know this, nobody knew. That night I got up to go and peep at the woman I desired.

I took the blanket with me, in case some help were needed. While I made my way to the rear of the kitchen where Marta usually slept, I laughed to myself. Walking along with a blanket over my shoulder was all that remained of my glorious past as a thief of young girls, a lover of great renown and many an opportunity. And I thought to myself

—*In the old days I covered them with my body, now I lay a blanket over them.*

I was chuckling to myself when I saw Vastsome Excellency pass by. He was walking stealthily, as if he didn't want to be seen. He was heading for the kitchen. He disappeared among some bushes. When I saw him again, he was talking to Marta. They were sitting close together. Was that them arguing? Yes, Marta was angry. Then suddenly, he put his hands on her shoulders as if to force her to lie down. Marta struggled. I immediately decided to intervene. But it's been a long time since I was of an age to carry things through. At the first step I took, I slipped and fell flat on the ground. I tried to get up but again got my legs in a tangle. When I finally managed to reach Marta, Vastsome had made his escape. The girl was sobbing. The moment she saw me, she raised her arm to show me she didn't want me to come near her. That scumbag had hurt the woman I adored.

Rage decided the matter for me: I had to snuff out that scoundrel's life. I lay in wait for him at the end of the corridor down which he would have to pass. When he drew level, I jumped on him with an unexpected force summoned from my past. I pushed him up against the wall and smashed the fellow's face against the stonework, then I smothered his snout with the blanket until he breathed his last.

That's exactly what happened, inspector. I was the one who took the mulatto's life. I killed for love. An old man like me is capable of love. He can love enough to kill.

8 Fourth day among the living

That morning, the policeman was determined to open a clearing in the labyrinth. At first light, he set off in the direction of the kitchen. He wanted to see if he could get into the storeroom to find out what was kept there. On the way, he came across Marta who was still sleeping. It was only when he came near that he noticed she was naked. The nurse awoke with a start, and the inspector showed he had good manners by averting his gaze. He apologised, and moved away so that she could make herself presentable. But she remained undressed and called to the policeman

—*Don't trouble yourself, I always do this . . .*

—*This?*

—*I sleep naked on the earth.*

He waited for Marta to cover herself. But she got up and, just as she was, without putting any clothes on, announced she was ready to talk. First, she justified herself: it wasn't because of fleas or rats. She slept outside because, for her, those rooms in the refuge were as sad as a coffin without a grave. And there was another reason too: she slept unclothed so that she could absorb the secret energies of the earth.

—*Even here, in this godforsaken place, I can still smell a perfume that comes from deep down in the world's belly.*

—*Maybe this perfume comes from you and not from the earth.*

—*Who knows? When I lie down like that, I feel like the earth's twin. Isn't that how the saying goes: a woman makes the earth into another woman?*

—*Marta, I want to ask you something. But answer me truthfully . . .*

—*Have I ever done otherwise?*

—*I . . . I want to know whether you had an affair with Vastsome Excellency.*

—*One affair, two affairs, many affairs . . .*

—*I mean it. I want to know whether you were lovers.*

She thought before replying. All of a sudden, she said —*I'm going to get dressed, I'll be back in a minute.* She went behind a wall taking only a brief moment. She reappeared, wearing only a *capulana*. This time she was offhand, her speech and movements brusque, without any warmth.

—*I've got to go and see old Navaia. He slept badly yesterday. You know him, the old man–child . . .*

—*Yes, he was the first to make a statement.*

—*Last night he nearly reached the end of his story. He was on the edge of death itself. I must go and see him.*

—*Wait, Marta,* said Izidine, blocking her way. —*You must answer me.*

—*Must? And why must I?*

—*Because I . . . I represent the authorities.*

—*Here, you have no authority.*

She dodged past the policeman and walked away. Izidine went after her and caught her by the arm. She stopped in her tracks next to him, so near that he was bathed in her breath. She tried to free herself. In vain. What happened was that her *capulana* fell to the ground revealing her woman's nakedness again. She picked up the cloth and hurriedly drew it about her.

—*Marta, you must answer. I'm doing my job.*

—*Get out of my way. I'm doing my job too.*

Once again, the nurse tried to escape. Izidine gripped her arm more firmly as it slid away from him. Then the inspector got angry.

—*Now, look here, you little district nurse. I'm not getting anywhere. And I know why. You're the one spoiling my enquiries . . .*

—*Me?*

—*Yes, you're the one filling the heads of these old codgers, so that they confuse me by talking a string of nonsense.*

—*It's not nonsense. You're the one who doesn't understand what they're saying.*

—*I don't understand?*

—*They're all telling you things of great importance. You just don't speak their language.*

—*I don't speak their language? But we always speak in Portuguese!*

—*But they speak another language, another Portuguese. And do you know why? Because they don't trust you. Let me just ask you this: why don't you stop being a policeman?*

—*Well, it just so happens I am a policeman, and that's why I'm here . . .*

—*There's no room for policemen here.*

—*Look, why are we having this stupid conversation? I'm here to find out who killed . . .*

—*That's all you want to do: find out who's guilty. But there are people here. They're old, they're at the end of their lives. But they're human beings, they're the bedrock of this same world you walk on over there in the city.*

—*Bedrock or no bedrock, they're not telling me all they know. Do you know what I'm going to do? I'm going to arrest the lot of them. They're all guilty, all accomplices.*

—*Well done. That's how you exert your authority. Congratulations, detective inspector sir, you'll be due for immediate promotion when you get back to Maputo.*

Marta Gimo wrapped her *capulana* more securely round her body. She sat down on a low wall. The policeman stuffed his hands in his pockets and turned his gaze towards the ocean. Only then did he notice what a beautiful day it was, the blue of the sky matching and rivalling that of the water. The peace of it all stretching away into the distance helped to calm him. He took a deep breath and sat down next to the nurse. When he spoke again, it was in a plaintive tone.

—*Please help me. I'm running out of time, I don't know what to do.*

Marta buried her face in her arms. By not answering him, she demonstrated her resistance. Her silence was greater than the inspector's patience. He pressed on.

—*What am I supposed to do? Tell me, you who are familiar with this world . . .*

—*You want to punish them!*

—*I want to get to the truth . . .*

—*You want to punish them, and do you know why? Because you're scared of them!*

—*Scared, me?*

—*Yes, scared. These old people are the past you are trampling on deep inside your head. These old people remind you of where you come from . . .*

Once again, fury got the better of him. Was the nurse looking for a fight? Well, he wasn't just any old policeman. If he wanted an answer, he'd get one. Just as he was honing his argument, he noticed that Marta was weeping. The woman's sudden weakness softened him. He placed his hand on her shoulder. But with a vigorous shake, she thrust his consoling gesture aside.

—*Leave me alone, you . . . policeman!*

Marta walked away. For a while, the inspector stayed where he was, gathering his thoughts. Then he decided to get on with the programme he had set himself. He made for the storeroom where the food supplies were kept. He stopped in front of all its locks, padlocks and bolts. Just when he was preparing to force the door, he was interrupted by Old Gaffer's voice

—*It would be better if you didn't go in there, sir.*

—*And why not?*

The old man hesitated before replying. Then he spoke in that peculiar way, his language couched in vagaries. He gave tongue to strange utterings.

—*That storeroom has lost its floor.*

—*It hasn't got a floor?*

Gaffer nodded. Inside, there was nothing but emptiness, an emptiness inside a hole. The floor had been swallowed up by the earth.

—*If you go in, you'll be swallowed up too.*

Izidine Naíta dismissed the old man's advice. With one blow he smashed the door's main lock. He cautiously peered inside before entering. It was dark and there was a strange, damp smell. Suddenly, a flapping of wings whipped through the silence and echoed through its depths. More wings beat the air, hitting Izidine hard in the face. He was knocked almost senseless to the ground. The door slammed shut. By this time, Izidine was no longer aware of what was happening. But I, the ghost inside him, felt Gaffer's hands helping him to his feet. And then the policeman was hauled before the witch.

9 Little Miss No's confession

I am Little Miss No, the witch. It is hard for me to summon up my memories. Don't ask me to unbury the past. Does the snake swallow its own saliva? Are you obliging me to talk? Very well. But mark my words, sir, people only pretend to obey. Don't try and order my soul around. If you do, only my body will talk.

Before anything else, let me say this: we shouldn't be talking like this at night. When we tell stories in the dark, we give birth to owls. By the time I finish my story, all the owls in the world will be perched on the tree you are leaning against. Aren't you scared? I know, even though you're black, you're from the city. You don't know about such things, nor do you have any time for them.

Let us now dig down into this cemetery. I mean it: cemetery. All those I loved are dead. My memory is a grave where I am gradually burying myself. My memories are dead beings, entombed in water rather than in the earth. I stir this water and everything turns red.

Do I fill you with fear? It was precisely for this reason, fear, that I was expelled from home. I was accused of witchcraft. It's a tradition back in our villages: an old woman risks being seen as a witch. I too was unfairly accused. I was blamed for deaths that had happened in our family. I was banished. I knew suffering. We women always live under the shadow of a knife: hindered from living when we are young, we are blamed for not dying when we grow old.

But nowadays, I take advantage of such accusations. It's convenient that they should think I'm a witch. In that way, they are frightened of me, they don't hit me or push me around. Don't you see? My powers are born out of a lie. All this has an explanation: my life has been a journey backwards, a sea that flows out into a river. Yes, I was my father's wife. Let me make myself clear. It wasn't I who slept with him. It was he who slept at me.

I must dwell a little on this recollection. I'm sorry, inspector, but I ought to remember my father. Why? Because I was the one who killed the mulatto, Excellency. Are you surprised? Well, let me explain right away: that monster had my father's spirit. I had to kill him because he was merely the instrument for carrying out the wishes of my late father. That's why, in order to talk of that Vastsome Excellency, I should first tell you about my father. Can I reminisce a while about him, on times gone by? I'm asking your permission because you began by issuing orders, even before I'd opened my mouth. I don't want to waste your time but you're not going to understand anything, sir, if I don't delve down deep into my memories. That's because things begin even before they happen.

My father was the victim of a curse. Every time he was

getting ready to make love he went blind. If he so much
as touched a woman's body, his sight would go. Weary of
this, my father consulted a witch doctor. He wasn't only
concerned about these passing periods of blindness. He
felt crushed by all the people round him. That was why he
decided to lay his life down on the soothsayer's mat. What
he was given were guarantees of wealth. The witch doctor
offered him promises: did my old man want the security
of abundance? Then he should take his eldest daughter,
that was me, and begin to make love to her. That was it:
to cross over from being father to husband, from being a
member of the family to being her lover.

—*Make love?* my father asked.

—*Yes, make love to her very self,* the soothsayer replied.

—*But supposing she doesn't accept me?*

—*She will, once she has taken the medicines I'm going to
give you.*

—*Aren't they dangerous?*

—*This medicine will remove her mouth from her heart. Your
daughter will accept you.*

—*And if not?*

—*If not . . . it's best we don't even think of it because in that
case, you'll have to die.*

My old man gulped dryness a good few times. Die?
Bewildered, he still had his doubts. But what could he do?
And so he complied. He went home and, lo and behold,
there I was to open the door, the daughter who was
destined for him. At that very moment, against the light of
the oil lamp, do you know what he saw? He saw all of
me. It was as if I were undressed.

—*My Little No: aren't you wearing any clothes?*

I could only laugh. No clothes? I pulled my *capulana* around me so that he could see what I was wearing. But in the hurry and confusion, my *capulana* came loose and revealed my breasts, my skin which, in those days, was capable of attracting fingers. At that point he ceased being able to see me. My father was losing his vision. That meant he had begun to desire me, his eldest daughter, just like any other woman. He studied the way forward with his hands, like a blind man. He tried to support himself against the door, but instead brushed my shoulders. And he felt me shudder.

—*Father, are you feeling all right?*

—*Help me in, I've just had too much darkness.*

The next day he gave me the potion the medicine man had prepared. I didn't even ask him what it was for. My eyes were full of doubt, and I just bowed my head. I didn't swallow the mixture straight away. I stood there thinking, as if I were trying to guess what would happen.

—*Can I drink it tomorrow?*

—*Yes, my daughter. Drink it when the desire strikes you.*

And so our love affair began. My father was in fact my first man. But I must admit to one thing: I never drank the potion. The witch doctor's gourd sat there for many years awaiting my lips. My old man believed I was under the influence of the spirits and attributed my behaviour to the medicine. The truth was that I was my only medicine.

So that was the life I led, as both wife and daughter, until my old father died. He hung himself out like a bat, drooping from a bare branch. The sun set. The frightful shadow of night fell. The hours went by, with him swaying in the darkness, the darkness swaying inside me. They didn't let me see him. In those days, children were forbidden to see the dead. You know, death is a type of nakedness: after you've seen it, you want to touch it. No image of my father remained with me, no trace of his presence. Following the old customs, the dead man's belongings, including photographs, were buried with him.

So I was left both an orphan and a widow. Now I'm old, wizened and as dark as the night when the owl went blind. A darkness that comes from sadness, not from race. But none of this matters, for each of us lives with sadnesses that are larger than mankind itself. But I have a secret which is mine alone. The old folk here know, but no one else. I'm going to tell it to you now, but not for you to write down anywhere. Listen well: every night I turn myself into water, I take the shape of liquid. That's why my bed is a bath tub. The old folk have even borne witness: I lie down and begin to perspire abundantly, so much so that my body is rendered down into sweat. I drain away into liquidescence. It is so painful to watch that the others withdraw in fear. No one was ever able to stay till the end when I vanished into transparency in the bath.

You don't believe me, sir? Come and watch, then. This very night, after this talk of ours. Are you scared? You've nothing to fear. For when morning comes, I immediately return to my former substance. First, my eyes take shape, like fish submerged in some makeshift aquarium. Then my mouth, my face and the rest are reformed. The hands, always stubborn when it comes to crossing the frontier, come last. They take longer every time. One of these days my hands will remain water. How good it would be not to come back!

To tell you the truth, I'm only happy when I'm my watery self. When I fall asleep in that state, I'm spared the trouble of dreaming. For water has no past. As far as a river is concerned, all that matters is today, like a wave on a permanent crest. There's a riddle that goes like this: 'What can you hit without ever hurting it?' Do you know the answer, sir?

I'll give you the answer: you can hit water without causing it an injury. In my case, life can deal me its blows when I'm water. If only I could live forever in liquid form, a wave falling on the beach, a river when it reaches its estuary, the sea in its infinity. No wrinkles, no pain, all of me cured of time. How I'd like to sleep and never return! But let's forget my ramblings. It wasn't for this that you ordered me to speak. All you want to know is what happened, isn't that so? Then I'll get back to the point.

That night I was on my way to my bath tub when I came across Old Gaffer and Sidimingo sleeping on the terrace. They were wrapped together for warmth. But at their age the mist wasn't good for them. I woke them up gently. Gaffer was the first to awaken. When he discovered old Mourão nestled up to him, he started shouting. He pushed Sidimingo roughly aside. The white man was startled.

—*What's this, Gaffer, are you mad?*

—*I thought you'd died.*

—And was that a good reason for pushing me like that?

I could understand Gaffer's fear. That old boy couldn't hold back his feelings. We can't let a person breathe his last in our arms, grow cold alongside our body. The dead clutch at our soul and drag us down to the depths with them. Here in this refuge, death is so common that I sometimes ask myself: what use are the dead? So many folk out there fertilizing the soil. Do you know why there are so many dead people piling up, inspector? For my part, I explain it like this: the dead are good for rotting this world's skin, this world which is like fruit with flesh and a stone deep inside it. The outer covering must fall off so that the inside can emerge. We, the living and the dead, are trying to unearth the stone which holds such astonishing wonderments. I'm sorry, inspector, I got carried away for no reason at all. I'll get back to the point, to that night when I met the two old men. I remember asking them

—So are you two going to stay here? To sleep out in the open air?

—Look, Little Miss No, let us stay right here, for today we don't feel like being with the old folk . . .

—I really must go and sleep in my bath tub. Otherwise I'd stay here too . . .

They both laughed, relieved to have got rid of me. Just like all the others, they too believed I was a witch. They assumed it was I who had planned the death of my husband in order to keep my children, and killed my children to have my grandchildren all to myself. Well, let them think what they liked.

That night, I lingered in the company of those two old men. I even saw Marta arrive and lie down, naked, on the ground. Gaffer and Mourão exchanged boyish confidences. That was when the mulatto director turned up. He summoned the three of us and told us to accompany him to his office. That was where he carried out his wicked acts. The three of us sat on a long bench and Gaffer was immediately the butt of harsh words.

—*What did I tell you to do, old man?*

The old blackman remained silent, his head hung low. He seemed to be ashamed, laden with guilt. Vastsome Excellency grasped his face and glared into it, his eyes flashing.

—*Didn't I tell you to cut that tree down?*

—*So is that what it was all about?* exclaimed the Portuguese in surprise. —*You were under orders from that scoundrel to cut my tree down!*

—*You shut your mouth too!*

The director was brief and to the point: Gaffer was declared guilty of insubordination then and there to be. Everyone knew the penalty that would follow. Salufo Tuco would be summoned to administer the corporal punishment. I even tried to placate the director's fury.

—*Excellency, you're surely not going to take it out on these poor folk . . .*

Then he turned on me. Shrieking all the time, he hit me on the chest. Once, then again, then repeatedly. He picked on my breasts: he rained blows down on them until I felt as if I were being torn asunder down the middle. Mourão and Gaffer tried to intervene but the poor old men, even together, couldn't make any impact. I lay flat out, pretending that this was merely a case of a man beating an old woman. Then Excellency turned to Gaffer and shouted

—*I told you to cut down that old Portugoose's tree and you disobeyed. Now you know . . .*

—*I know. But let me ask you one thing: don't call anyone to come and beat me.*

Then, turning to the old Portuguese, Gaffer begged

—*Please, you give me the beating.*

—*Beat you? Are you out of your mind?*

—*I don't want a black man to beat me.*

—*Don't ask me to do that, Gaffer. I can't, I haven't got it in me.*

At that moment, the director cut in. He asked the white man, his voice laden with sarcasm

—*Don't tell me you've never taken it out on a black. Hey, boss?*

He laid great stress on the word 'boss'. Gaffer, to our surprise, joined in along with Excellency.

—*Yes, please do as I ask, boss.*

—*I don't understand, Gaffer: am I your 'boss' now?*

It was the director of the refuge who answered. The conversation seemed to amuse him. He sat down in his chair with an authoritative air. Then he swaggeringly pointed a judge's finger.

—*Yes, you whites never left off being the bosses. We blacks . . .*

—*What do you mean, we blacks? Keep your mouth shut, you self-seeking scumbag!*

The old Portuguese was getting carried away. The hint

of a smile appeared in the corner of Vastsome Excellency's mouth.

—*Keep my mouth shut? If that's what the boss tells me.*

—*I'm no one's boss!*

—*You are, you're my boss!* Gaffer insisted.

—*For heaven's sake, I'm not a boss! Don't give me that stuff and nonsense. I'm Domingos Mourão, that's all I fucking well am!*

The Portuguese, now at boiling point, was pacing up and down, all the while repeating —*I'm Domingos Mourão, I'm Sidimingo, for heaven's sake!* Suddenly Old Gaffer threw himself in the white man's path. Bowing his head, he begged in an undertone

—*Please, Mourão. Give me a beating.*

—*I can't.*

—*You won't hurt me, I promise.*

—*It'll hurt me, Gaffer.*

—*Please, Sidimingo. Do it for me, my brother.*

The white man closed his eyes. He looked as if he was on the verge of tears. Slowly, he gripped the whip. Still with his eyes shut, he drew back his arm. But he didn't get as far as carrying out the sentence. For suddenly, outside, a storm tore through the skies. Lightning flashes and thunderclaps merged with one another. Never before had I witnessed such fury from the firmaments. I took some *kwangula* leaves from my bag. I gave a bunch to each of the old men to hold, and so prevent their lungs from bursting. I gave one to everyone except the director. Then I gave the order

—*Keep quiet: the* wamulambo *is passing across the sky.*

—*The* wamulambo? asked the director, his voice shaking.

—*Quiet, you devil-worshipper!*

The director rushed out, under pressure from his bowels. Sidimingo was getting alarmed. He wasn't acquainted with all our beliefs. He didn't know about the *wamulambo*, the huge snake that slithers through the sky during a storm. We remained for some time, our hearts cowering, until the cyclone grew tired. Then, we went outside to look at the sky. There were no more peals of thunder. But the refuge was strewn with damage. Tin roofs had been ripped off. Old Gaffer spoke.

—*I've been telling them for ages to paint those roofs . . .*

The old man was right. Those serpents that appeared in storms had confused the glistening undulations of the tin roofs with waves on the water. This was why they had halted all of a sudden high above, to then plunge onto the sheets of tin.

—*Miss No, you who are a witch, could surely give your old Sidimingo here a* wamulambo.

—*Let me tell you something, white man: never wish for a snake like that. They help their owners, but in return, they always ask for blood . . .*

The Portuguese didn't even smile half-heartedly. It's incredible how an old man depends on the state of the weather, how he becomes more frail depending on the forecast. Now, each one of us old folk felt it was our most vulnerable point. Mourão was the one who was most affected by the weight of the clouds. He looked at the firmament and said

—*The sky is enough to make the Virgin run for shelter.*

My breasts were seized by unbearable pain. They seemed to be bleeding. I hurriedly separated myself from my companions. I went off to my house to lie down. I badly needed to turn myself into water. I opened the door and saw the bath tub smashed to pieces: the storm had taken its revenge on it. Was it the *wamulambo* confronting me, punishing me for my lies? I sat there, dejected. The blood soaked my blouse.

I stayed in that tiny room watching my breasts drip blood. Never again would I suckle my grandchildren, whether they were truly mine or merely of my flesh. Milk cannot flow from where blood has come. I cursed the mulatto, wishing him all manner of deaths. And let me tell you this: Vastsome Excellency's fate was sealed there and then. I was the one who sent him on his way, I was the author of his sudden departure. That same blood that oozed from my breast, he would lose from his body.

Life is a house with two doors. There are some who come in through the first door and are afraid to open the second one. They wander round the house marking time. Others decide to open the back door through an act of will. That was what I did at that moment. I turned the cupboard door key in its lock, and my life swayed on the edge of the abyss.

In front of me I saw the sandalwood box I had kept for so many years. From it, I took the root of that shrub that grows next to mangroves. I opened my legs and deliberately drove the root into the centre of my body, through the gap where I and life had first come face to face with each other. I waited for the poison to spread

through my insides. My strength sapped, I staggered back
to my friends.

—*What's wrong, Little Miss No?*

—*I've come to say goodbye.*

The Portuguese smiled: in which no particular
direction was I going? Gaffer laughed too. But then they
saw how sad I was.

—*Do you know the storm broke my bath tub?*

—*Don't start going on about that business of the water, Miss
No*, replied Sidimingo.

I was still able to smile. No one's knowledge is
complete: but how whites glorify their ignorance! For the
Portuguese, the matter was cut and dry. A person turning
into water? Impossible! One's body fragments after death,
dissolves into nothingness, into the compaction of a piece
of bone. I didn't have the strength to argue with him. I
picked up a handful of sand and let the grains slip through
my fingers.

—*Tonight, as I have no bath tub, I'm going to slip away
through these sands . . .*

As far as I was concerned, that was to be my last night.
I was going to be buried like rain, shattered into a
thousand drops. All of a sudden, the Portuguese shook me
anxiously.

—*Your legs are covered in blood, Little Miss No. What's the
matter?*

—*It's blood from my breast, because of that mulatto who hit me.*

—*No, Little Miss No, this blood is the work of another.*

—*What have you done to yourself?* asked the old black
man.

Old Gaffer knew. Being black, he was familiar with our customs. In his clumsy way, he explained to the Portuguese that I was killing myself. There was only one way to save me. That was for one of them to make love to me.

—*But isn't that risky? Couldn't the poison be passed on to us?*

The two old fellows silently exchanged fears and anxieties. They looked at the ground without speaking. Then Old Gaffer smiled and spoke: the white man needn't worry. He would take care of the matter. At which point the Portuguese challenged him.

—*But it's deadly dangerous, Gaffer.*

—*If you want to catch the locust, you can't be afraid of the earth's dirt.*

—*You know, Gaffer, I'm the one who's going to do this!*

—*Don't even think about it, my white friend. This is for me.*

And they argued between themselves. Did they both want me? They presented their credentials and everything: one of them had more certainties than arguments, the other was of the right race. The black man said: go to bed with the witch and your fate's more certain than that of straw in a fire. The Portuguese fell silent for a moment. His voice was seized by a stammer. Then he let it all out.

—*I didn't want to tell you this, but . . .*

Then he was quiet again. He seemed to have lost his nerve.

—*Speak, man!*

—*It's just that Little Miss No, in her day, raised her skirt many a time for me. I've seen her without any clothes on.*

I felt sorry for Domingos Mourão. The Portuguese
hadn't understood the reason why I had shown him my
body. Mourão still didn't know many of our secrets. When
an old woman strips off her clothes and challenges a man,
it's a sign of rage. That moment which Sidimingo had
assumed to be one of courting was in fact an expression
of scorn. Poor fellow, the old white man didn't deserve it.
It was too late to explain things, and better to allow
Mourão his illusions.

The dispute was eventually resolved in the black man's
favour. Old Gaffer took my hand as if he were my lover.
He pointed to my house and asked

—*Shall we go?*

I had already forgotten the art of exchanging caresses. I
was even more confused by Gaffer's talk. —*This is the mat
and it's only a mat when one person alone sleeps on it. But when
two lovers lie down, it takes the weight of the world upon it.*
—*You say beautiful things, Gaffer. But apart from your talk, do
you still do beautiful things?* Old Gaffer continued to unravel
his speech. —*Take Navaia Caetano,* he said. —*Is he an old
man or a child? Listen to me, my Little Miss No. Have you
never seen a mulatto? Well, then? If you can be a mixture of
races, you can be a mixture of ages. You are an old–young girl
child, my sweet little one.*

His whisperings in my ear encouraged me to be
reckless, convinced me that I was still in the flower of my
youth. I already knew that old age doesn't give us any
extra wisdom, it just allows other illusions. My illusion
was to believe Old Gaffer. That I was the most beautiful,
the most womanly woman. And so we went to it, our

bodies by now free of clothes. Suddenly, he stopped.

—*I'm scared*.

—*Scared?*

—*I've always been scared*.

—*What if I give you a bit of a fondle?* I asked. And that's just what I did. My hand wandered over his fragile private parts. He smiled and replied that it wasn't worth it.

—*It's as hopeless as trying to get rust off a nail*.

We laughed. Life is the worst of all bandits: we know our existence is punctuated by fear and surprise attacks. Just as Old Gaffer was about to sow the feelings of his heart, Vastsome Excellency appeared. He came in without knocking and stood there watching, one corner of his mouth turned up in a smirk.

—*Well, just look at this, what a pair of lovebirds we have here.*

Pushing Gaffer, he kicked him aside and told him

—*Get out of here you old motherfucker!*

Gaffer went out through the door. Then Vastsome pretended to court me. He played the wooing rooster. He humiliated me like an animal. I pretended to go along with the mulatto's deception, as if I accepted his courtship. And I managed to soften his expression as I soothed his shoulders with my hands.

—*I've got a special little drop of liquor . . .*

That was what he wanted. I filled a glass for him. Excellency drank it and drank more again. Until a fit of dizziness laid him out on the ground. At that point I went and lay on top of him. Just like that, naked and moist, I fitted myself round his body like a concave mirror.

Excellency embraced me. His kisses sweated the frothy heat from the drink. The man flitted from one name to another in his deception.

—*Marta! Tina . . . my Ernestina!*

He completed his virile favours inside me. Groaning like an animal, he finished. I separated myself from him, eager for my ablutions. It was as if his liquids, inside me, were souring me more than the previous poison. In the mirror I again noticed the blood on my breast. While I was washing myself, the mulatto shouted, demanding more drink.

I returned to the room and once again filled his glass. There was a trace of blood on its rim. The director didn't notice the red fingerprint on the glass. He drank the poison in one gulp and patting his stomach, ordered

—*Fill it up again, old woman!*

The glass fell to the ground and smashed. And Vastsome Excellency's body collapsed heavily on top of the thousand shards of crystal.

10   *Fifth day among the living*

Izidine wandered around all day with the image of the witch gnawing away at his thoughts. He had been very struck by how thin she was. The others said the only food Little Miss No ate was salt. She carried water up from the sea and poured it into hollows in the rocks. She would wait for the water to evaporate and then lick the bottom of these hollows.

The morning was moist, for it had rained during the night. The clouds had opened while he was listening to the witch. Was it mere coincidence? The policeman strolled across the yard until his attention was drawn by the old folk shouting. He went over to them. The inmates of the refuge were dancing around the frangipani. Navaia Caetano was climbing the trunk and catching little furry creatures which he handed to the others. At that time of year, every time it rains, tree trunks are covered with caterpillars called *matumanas* The old folk were eating these caterpillars. Even Izidine knew the custom. The nurse joined him to watch the scene. The policeman took pleasure in showing he too was familiar with the tradition.

—*They're not the same caterpillars*, she corrected him.

—*If they're not the same, they're similar.*

—*That's what you think. Ask them what they dream of after eating these* matumanas.

—*You tell me.*

—*They'll tell you that butterflies flutter from their eyes while they sleep.*

They said this and more: that the insects grew inside them, turning into sturdy butterflies, made from their own flesh. While the butterflies escaped through their eyes, they themselves grew thin, empty, until only their bones were left. Laughing, they concluded —*It's not we who eat the creatures. It's they who eat us.* The milky juices of the *matumanas* were causing them to give free rein to their imagination.

—*I hope there's one at least who hasn't eaten* matumanas. *Otherwise, there'll be no one to give me a statement.*

—*Perhaps it'll loosen their tongues. Have you never heard of the truth drug?*

Marta Gimo smiled and excused herself. She had to go about her business. The inspector waved goodbye and went over to the tree. He thought he would join the old folk in catching caterpillars. Might he not even gain their trust by doing this? But just as he was about to catch his first *matumana*, a voice ordered him to stop.

—*You can't come near . . .*

—*Why?*

—*Because you can't . . .*

Annoyed, he obeyed. The old people didn't accept him. The policeman couldn't even get near them. How could he expect them to open up and tell him the truth? The thought, while obvious, left him depressed. He took himself off to his room and shut himself away from the world, until Old Gaffer came to see him in the late afternoon. He knocked on the door, came in and sat down before even being invited.

—*We don't trust you, inspector.*

—*But why? Just because I'm a policeman?*

He shrugged his shoulders and mumbled some vague excuses. Strange things were happening at the refuge. The country had become a dangerous place for those who sought the truth. And then there were other reasons that they, the elders, had weighed up carefully.

—*Is it because, in your view, I'm not a good man?*

—*You are neither good nor bad. You just don't exist.*

—*What do you mean, I don't exist?*

—*Were you ever circumcised?*

The inspector was lost for an answer. He was astonished. So was that it? Or was it just an excuse, just one more way of throwing dust in his face? Whatever it was, he ought to be able to get past that unexpected hurdle. So he prepared himself to be subjected to ceremonies.

—*Are you going to circumcise me?*

The old man laughed. He was already an adult. But as for a ceremony, yes, he would go through one. It was a condition for acceptance into the family, the community of elders. What was more, it would be that very night if he so wished. Izidine gave his consent. The policeman was on the verge of despair, seeing time slipping, sand like, between his fingers. So they came to an agreement. Old Gaffer went to tell the others to prepare the ritual.

Some hours later there was a knock on the door. In came Old Gaffer, Mourão and Navaia. The policeman was ordered to take all his clothes off.

—*So you're going to cut me after all?* he asked anxiously.

—*Sit down here in the middle.*

Old Gaffer produced one of Marta's dresses. They held the policeman by his waist and stuffed the dress over his head. The policeman looked at himself in disbelief, dressed in woman's clothes.

—*At this party, you're going to pretend you're a woman.*

They began to chant, to beat their drums and dance. Old Gaffer encouraged him to dance and sing in womanly ways. Izidine performed as best as he could. The old timers roared with laughter. Then they went out and the policeman accompanied them as far as the courtyard. Tired, he lay down on the paving stones, exposed to the coolness of the evening. He closed his eyes but opened them straight away. He was woken by someone's footsteps. It was Marta. She stopped, puzzled by the policeman's attire. Izidine sat up, rubbed his face with his hands, wiping away his embarrassment. He told her what had happened and she burst out laughing.

—*They were having fun at your expense. And at the expense of my dress.*

—*I'm sorry, Marta.*

—*Come with me. It's a beautiful night for two women to go for a walk.*

They strolled as far as the frangipani tree. Marta

pointed to lights that were being lit along the beach,
down by the water's edge.

—*They are torches. The old folk light them so as to catch
lobsters.*

The lights were floated out on the waves and cast a
reddish glow over the foam. Marta seemed to be in the
mood for poetry. She said that light weighs less than
water, and its reflections pitch and toss on the waters like
fish carved out of moonlight, like seaweed fashioned by
fire.

—*The memories of those old people are like that too, floating
lighter than time.*

The inspector's attention was drawn to a strange bulge
in the dress he was wearing. He pulled at the padded
object: it was another scale. He showed it to the nurse.

—*Do you know what this is?*

—*That, my dear inspector . . .*

—*Call me Izidine.*

—*That, Izidine, is an anteater's scale, the* halakavuma . . .

—*Ah! I know. The one that comes down from the clouds to
predict the future?*

—*So you haven't forgotten our tradition after all. Let's see if
you've forgotten anything else . . .*

And she passed her hand over his face, descending
caressingly over his chest. Was that his dress she was
unbuttoning? Her gesture invited him to come even
closer. She seemed to want to tell him a secret. She placed
her lips upon his ear, but rather than utter words, she
imitated the sound of the sea within a shell. Then, with
her arm, she made him lie down.

—*The old timers can't see us, can they?*

Marta smiled and rolled over so that he was on top of her. Izidine tried to protect her by placing his hands under her. But she declined such consideration.

—*Put your hands to better use, I'm well-cushioned.*

Had the policeman ever experienced such softness? And I, Ermelindo Mucanga, dwelling in the lover's body, suddenly saw myself drifting away from such visions. The truth is that I was beginning to fall passionately for Marta Gimo myself. And a night spirit is forbidden to get involved in matters of the living. So I let myself fall into a void, no longer aware of myself or the world. Everything went dark until I saw Izidine once more, getting up and walking away from the nurse. The policeman stretched his arm out to adjust his dress. He looked over at the beach: there were no longer any torches.

—*The old folk aren't on the beach any more.*

—*No. They're up there now.*

Marta pointed to the stars in the sky. The policeman was lost among the heavenly bodies that glimmered overhead, imagining them to be torches carried by the old people. And he rested in silence, until she asked

—*Do you know what I hated most about that mulatto?*

—*About who?*

—*Him, Excellency.*

—*What was that?*

—*When Salufo Tuco died, we asked for his body to be taken to Maputo for burial. Yet again the mulatto refused.*

Marta would watch the helicopter coming and going, going and coming. They brought in boxes and left empty.

On a number of occasions she had asked them to take sick people back with them. Excellency always refused.

—*When it came down to it, they were scared.*

—*Scared? Scared of what?*

—*They were scared we would spill the beans once we got out . . .*

The inspector was suddenly interested. Possibly too much so. He shone the torch near her face. He wanted to know who 'they' were. And what were the beans they might spill. The nurse dodged away from the beam of light.

—*You'll never understand. What's happening here is a coup d'état.*

—*A coup d'état?*

—*Yes, and that's what you should be worrying about, mister policeman.*

—*But here in the fort, a coup? Izidine laughed in disbelief.*
—*Honestly, Marta . . .*

—*It's not just here in the fort. It's throughout the country. Oh yes, it's a coup against the past.*

Once again, Marta Gimo had caught him on the wrong foot. This time the policeman avoided an argument. He let her speak. And that's exactly what she did.

—*We must preserve the past. Otherwise, the country will be left without its bedrock.*

—*I agree entirely, Marta. I just want to know who killed Vastsome Excellency. That's all.*

The conversation ended. The inspector was getting ready to return to his room when he was stopped by Marta's peals of laughter. The nurse was amused at the sight of him, solemn and self-important, dressed in women's clothes. He waved his arm, turned on his heel, and bowed low to her. Marta approached to bid him goodnight. She unwrapped some papers and handed them to him.

    —*Read this.*

    —*What is it?*

    —*A letter. Read it.*

    —*A letter? Who from?*

    —*From Ernestina.*

11 *Ernestina's Letter*

I am Ernestina, Vastsome Excellency's wife. Correction:
Vastsome's widow. I am writing these lines on the eve of
being taken to the city, and while they are ferreting
around all over the fort. They will never find my
husband's body. When they've finished their search, they'll
take me away with them. I shall leave like one disqualified,
assumed to be a helpless soul. They won't ask me for a
statement, or even for my feelings. I prefer to be an
outcast like this. Let no one pay me any attention or take
me for a fool. I don't even know why I'm writing this
letter, or to whom. But I want to write it, I want to
breach this wall that hems me in. For years I lived
surrounded by old people, folk who are waiting for their
quick and certain end. Isn't death an end without finality?

Vastsome died in mysterious circumstances. He didn't
even get a burial. It was better like that: I was saved the
hypocrisy of a funeral. It's not the first time my life's path
has crossed with death. My only child died at birth. I
would never again be able to have children. When this
misfortune took place, I was separated from Vastsome. I
had thought this separation would become permanent.

Vastsome had been appointed to run the refuge at São Nicolau. I refused to go with him. Our relationship had spent itself, and I had become exhausted by one disappointment after another. But my son's death had left me weak and vulnerable. That was when I decided to make things up with Vastsome and join him. They say that women who see their children die become blind. I can understand what they mean: it's not that they stop seeing things. What happens is that they stop seeing time. When the past becomes invisible, it stops hurting.

During the war, I suffered most from things I didn't witness. The atrocities that happened! I was told that Vastsome showed no mercy on the field of battle, behaving just like the enemy he called devils. I listened to reports of massacres as if they had taken place in another world. As if it were all a dream. And dreams are like clouds: only their shadows belong to us. All I possessed were fleeting shadows on the earth. I listened to the rumours about my husband. And I wept. I wept every time I ate. Food and tear drops mingled on my lips, and I swallowed so many confused and twisted sadnesses. My life tastes of salt. That's why I'm in a hurry to get away from these beaches. To forget, forever, the taste of the sea.

When I got to the refuge, I came face to face with my husband's wickedness. Excellency was selling the provisions destined for the refuge. The old folk weren't even being fed the basic necessities and so they were wasting away. Sometimes I had the impression they were dying skewered by their very bones. But Vastsome really did not care about their suffering.

—How can you possibly do nothing about it, you who are always talking 'in the name of the people' . . .

—The old people are used to not eating anything, he would answer. *—If they start eating now, it might even be bad for them . . .*

How could Vastsome have stooped so low? In the beginning, I had even loved that man. His body was my country. I gave him names of my own, names I invented with the strength of my love for him. But I never revealed these names to him. They remained with me, secrets I hid even from myself. I didn't believe he would know how to care for adornments created for him by my affection. That was when I first experienced a desire to distance myself from Vastsome. At first, it wasn't true. I was like the river which, only in an illusion, leaves its source behind.

In time, though, Vastsome's true nature was confirmed. As old Navaia says: we don't discover anything; things just reveal themselves. Time brought me that man's real face. God forgive me, but I stopped loving him. More than that: I began to hate him. At that moment, I still wanted an explanation for my anger. Today, I need no reason at all to hate him.

And I discovered a means to justify myself: Vastsome had served in the war. He had taken part in campaigns I would rather not know about. He saw many people die. Who knows whether it wasn't during such experiences that his last trace of kindness was extinguished? What was strange was that most people had been rendered homeless by the armed conflict. In Vastsome's case, the opposite occurred: it was war that had been made homeless and so it lodged inside him, a refugee in his heart. And now, how was such wickedness to be expunged from deep within him?

It was during the war that Vastsome Excellency came to know Salufo Tuco, the man who would later become our servant. Salufo had already served as a soldier during colonial times. He was a strange man, but a kind one. No one would have believed his real age. He didn't look more than fifty. Yet he must have been well over seventy, looking as he did still quite youthful.

His clothes were made up of little pieces of cloth, patches sewn roughly together. He dressed like this to conjure up memories of his early youth. He recalled his first paid job as a very young tailor's assistant. His boss was an Indian who paid him his wages in remnants of cloth rather than money. By dressing in patches, was Salufo returning to the lost paradise of his childhood? I don't know. I asked him once, but he denied it. This was his reply: can a snake move back into the skin it has shed?

I don't know what had happened on the battlefield but Salufo had strange ties of loyalty to Vastsome. He became his right-hand man. Salufo was the one who unloaded the cargo brought in by the helicopters. The old folk always tried to help, curious to know what came in the boxes. But Vastsome Excellency never allowed it. Only Salufo was allowed to handle these loads. He alone could carry them on his back to the storeroom which is always locked and bolted. The storeroom is really the fort's old chapel. If it was once a holy place, it is even more so now. The old chapel is subject to a thousand restrictions, converted as it is into a store for merchandise. No one except for Vastsome Excellency could go in there. And Salufo Tuco, when authorized. As far as I was concerned, the explanation was an easy one: my husband didn't want people to know the real amount of food, blankets and soap that were being sent. Vastsome didn't want people's eyes prying into things their hands would never touch.

Salufo did our household chores. I enjoyed his company. Inside his gigantic body lay hidden a gentle soul. Salufo would confide in me a lot. There was a constant complaint in his words: he lamented the living conditions of the old people in the refuge. And he said that in villages out in the country, the elderly led a far happier life. The family protected them, and they were listened to and respected. The elders had the last word in the gravest matters. Salufo recalled the old days and his face took on a boyish expression. Then, once he had finished, he shut himself away in his melancholy.

One day, Salufo Tuco told me he had decided to run away. I was sad: I was not only going to lose an employee but also a friend. But he was adamant. And he asked me not to say anything to Vastsome. In spite of my sadness, I promised to keep quiet.

—*But how are you going to get past all the mines?*

—*I'm a soldier, I know the secrets of war. I know how mines are laid and taken up.*

His plan was to take with him all the old people who were tired of the refuge. He had already spoken to them in secret. Almost all of them agreed to join the escape. Only half a dozen had declined. Were they too frightened to take a risk? Or had death taught them to be resigned to their insignificant fate?

As the time for the planned escape approached, I was seized by growing anxiety. One slip by Salufo could drag many of those old people to their death. I called him and begged

—*Salufo, don't leave like this, unprepared.*

—*What should I do, madam?*

—*I've been thinking. Ask Little Miss No, for she can bless your journey.*

—*A light-skinned lady like you, madam, with such a Portuguese soul, do you believe in such things?*

—*I do, Salufo.*

Maybe he only did it to please me, but Salufo agreed. That same afternoon he went to consult the old witch. I don't know what they talked about. I only know that Miss No turned up at my house that night. To my surprise, she took both my hands and begged me.

—*Ernestina, don't let him leave. The truth is . . . I'm not really a witch.*

—*Aren't you?*

—*I never have been. I have no powers, Ernestina.*

Her body seemed to be asking for some comfort. But her voice showed no sign of weakness. Even so, I consoled her.

—*You have powers, I know it.*

—*How do you know?*

—*It's something only another woman knows.*

Miss No shook her head. I don't know whether she was denying my words or her past full of lies. While the band of fugitives were making their final preparations, I noticed Miss No praying, imploring in a low voice

—*Don't go, Salufo, I beg you in Christ's name!*

But Salufo was committed to leaving with the rest. He had waited for the cover of night, out of respect for the witch's request. She had told him: a traveller should never leave at dusk. Salufo led the group of old folk and waved his stick before being swallowed up by the gloom. They bade farewell to the refuge by unleashing an eery 'ouooh' sound. Later, I found out why. They were imitating the hoot of an owl. That noise was to foretell Vastsome Excellency's fate.

Anxious, I stayed awake the whole night. I was scared I'd hear explosions at any moment. If one of the old people stepped on a mine, the bang would echo across the grassy plains. I was listening so hard that I wasn't even aware that Vastsome wasn't at home. I surprised him on his return, as he tiptoed in when day was almost breaking. He got a fright when he saw me sitting on the veranda.

—*Tina! What are you doing?*

—*Nothing, I couldn't get to sleep inside.*

—*I've been to see . . .*

—*It doesn't matter, Vast, don't talk. I didn't ask anything.*

The night had then passed without incident. The old ones had got past the minefield. I shut myself away in this room, indifferent to everything and everybody. Marta still came to visit me a few times. But I had nothing to say. She would hold my arms in silence. And we would stand there looking into each other's eyes as if contemplating the endless depths of the ocean.

★ ★ ★

Two months later, however, Salufo Tuco returned. He was
sad and in rags. He arrived and settled in without saying a
word to anybody. He went back into the store cupboard
he used as a room and resumed his daily tasks as if
nothing at all had occurred. I asked him what had
happened. He didn't answer. He took his time over
invented chores. Only at the end of the day did he sit
down and talk. He was deeply hurt. The world out there
had changed. No one respected old people any more. It
was all the same whether you were living in a refuge or
outside. In other homes for the elderly, the situation was
even worse than in São Nicolau. Relatives and soldiers
came in from outside to help themselves to food. The old
folk who before had yearned for company, no longer
looked forward to their visits.

—*We put up with the war, now we're going to have to put up
with peace.*

Salufo explained it like this: everywhere else, members
of the family brought gifts to comfort those who were in
homes. In our country it was the other way round.
Relatives visited the old to steal things from them. To the
greed of entire families, one had to add that of soldiers
and new officials. Everybody came to take the food, soap
and clothes intended for the old. There were international
organizations that gave money to support social welfare.
But this money never reached the elderly. Everyone had
turned into goats. And as the saying goes – a goat eats
wherever it is tethered.

When Salufo Tuco told his friends in the refuge about

this, they didn't want to believe him. They told him he
was making it up to discourage them from leaving. Salufo
answered them: you are the orange peel on which there is
no fruit left. The rulers of our land have squeezed
everything dry. Now they're squeezing the peel to see if
they can still extract some juice.

Then Salufo Tuco stopped bringing the subject up. He
refused to recall what had happened during those two
months away from São Nicolau. And I could understand.
Salufo had got by, living with some nephews of his on the
basis of a lie. The old man had made it known he had
wealth and possessions. Just so that the young ones would
look after him. Salufo exchanged a lie for a corner in
someone's home. Sick of that world, he decided to return
to São Nicolau.

—*I prefer to be trodden on by Excellency.* And he added,
half laughing: —*So that I can be comforted later by his
lady . . .*

And now, Salufo, what are you going to do? This was
the question I should have asked him. But I preferred to
keep quiet. Why torture him? Salufo seemed to sense my
doubt. He got up and said

—*I've been a soldier. Do you know what I'm going to do?*

He explained his extraordinary plan to me: he was
going to plant mines again round the fort. He would bury
the same mines that were being dug up along the road.

—*They're clearing mines. I'm going to start unclearing them
again.*

I couldn't believe what I was hearing. Everything
seemed so unreal that I couldn't even find any questions

to ask. How would the old man get hold of explosives?

—*I brought them with me, I stole them. No one saw me.*
They're unplanting them over there, I'll plant them again here.

—*But Salufo, you . . .*

—*Now this is going to be a proper fortress!*

—*Are you mad, Salufo?*

—*No madam. They're the ones who are crazy.*

—*But what for? Why lay mines, Salufo?*

—*I saw the world out there. I don't want anyone to come and
disturb us here.*

—*But who . . . is going to come here?*

—*They'll get here, Mrs Tina. They'll come here when they
run out of pasture out there in the cities.*

I knew only too well what Salufo was saying. I had
been in the city and had witnessed the covetousness of
the rich. Nowadays, everything was allowed, every type of
opportunism, all manner of disloyalty. Everything was
turned into pasture, cud to be eaten, chewed and digested
in growing paunches. And all this was taking place
alongside the direst poverty.

Salufo Tuco wanted to shut off the road to the future.
And he didn't just talk about it. He devoted himself to
this strange mission with heart and soul. He would tell
Vastsome Excellency he was going out into the
surrounding countryside to pick a bit of greenery, some
nkakana leaves for Miss No's herbal medicine. Vastsome
appeared to believe him. Either that or he was pretending.
For it was a deadly game. One day, the old man would be
blown to pieces. Salufo would shake his huge hand in the
air when my husband was pretending to warn him.

—*I'm immune to mines, boss. Don't forget I was once a* naparama, *my body was sealed by witchcraft from the effect of bullets.*

Early each morning, before the sun was up, he would go out with a sack and a hoe. —*I'm going to do some planting, the earth gets angry if we don't plant anything. The fields grow bitter when men abandon them.* Vastsome Excellency, his hands stuffed in his pockets, looked amused as he watched his servant walk off. Salufo even called back, insisting.

—*It's true, boss: this wretchedness is the earth's revenge.*

One morning, I was awoken by Vastsome's voice. It was still twilight. My late husband was remonstrating with Salufo in the storeroom. I got up to have a look. I interrupted their quarrel.

—*What's wrong, Vast?*

—*This sonofabitch opened the store.*

Then he ordered me to leave. It wasn't an argument for women to see. And indeed it wasn't. Ignoring my presence, Vastsome grabbed the old man by his patches and demanded an explanation for what he had stolen. Salufo had no time to answer. Vastsome's fist was already crashing with all its strength into his mouth. Salufo fell. Kicks rained down on him. Salufo's body leapt at the command of every blow. Vastsome was beside himself. I shouted, begged him to leave the man alone. Finally, he paused in his beating and, breathless, stammered

—*I'm going to see what you took. Just you wait, my little scumbag.*

Salufo Tuco didn't die there and then. When Excellency

left him stretched out and motionless, he was still
breathing. But his body was already paralysed. He asked
me to call the other old people. I rushed off. When they
gathered round Salufo, the old folk were astonished by his
request.

—*Tie me to the vanes on the windmill!*

They hesitated, perplexed. But then they obeyed. Salufo
was always talking about the windmill. He would fix his
gaze on the vanes as they turned, and become intoxicated
by their movement. And he would say: that wind there is
all made by hand. I may have forgotten their reasons but
the old folk agreed to his request and took him up to the
top. Nor do I know how they managed to climb the stairs
in the windmill carrying that dead weight. They lashed
him to the vanes of the mill. His arms and legs spread
wide. Just as he wanted: with only the sky above him and
waiting for the winds to blow. For days, our skies hadn't
been visited by even the slightest breeze.

Whether by magic or coincidence, at that very
moment, the winds blew and the mill's vanes began to
turn. The old man turned too, like the hand of a clock.
Down on the ground, we grew distressed, watching Salufo
Tuco on that merry-go-round. But he seemed to be
enjoying himself. He was shrieking with laughter even
when he was upside down. Some time passed and then he
fell silent, his eyes wide open. It looked to me as if he had
fainted. All of a sudden, the wind stopped. Salufo was still,
like a flag at rest. The sky he yearned for so much seemed
to have entered his eyes. That was when Vastsome
Excellency appeared. He was coming from the direction

of the storeroom, more furious than a wild beast. He was huffing spittle and puffing spume. His eyes flashed when he saw Salufo hanging on the vanes. We couldn't understand why that person, tied there high above us, could make him so angry. He bellowed an order for him to be untied and brought down.

That's what they did. When they placed his body on the ground, Salufo was already dead. Excellency struck the body in his frustration. Then, mouthing oaths, he walked off. Yet I hesitated to go with him. I owed greater loyalty to Salufo. So I joined the other old people who were standing round their dead friend. Fearfully, I leaned over him. Then I noticed the strange way the dead man contemplated us. It was as if his whole body had died, but not his glance. That was precisely it: his eyes were still alive. The old folk looked at him in disbelief. Old Gaffer was the only one who was not surprised.

—*But aren't there living people who have dead eyes?*

He was referring to the blind. According to him, it was natural for there to be dead people with live eyes. I changed the subject. There were more urgent matters.

—*What shall we do with him?*

The old people were uncertain over which final rites they should give the dead body. For Salufo gave the impression that he was a hot coal beneath the ashes. Who could be sure of his definitive state of being? And so they remained there, waving to him, talking to him and telling him jokes. Until, in the end, they took him to be buried far away from there. I stood, motionless, as if rooted to the ground. For some time after, I could still hear Salufo's peals of laughter, like the echo of time itself.

They told me later that in the place where they buried him, the buzzing of flies could be heard coming from the depths of the earth. Yes, those flies must have gone to the grave along with Salufo. And whoever passed by that place could hear the insects buzzing underground. Others said it was Salufo Tuco snoring away in his final resting place.

That's all. I can already hear the voices of those who are coming to fetch me. I'm going to close this letter, enclosing myself in it. This is my last letter. Before that, I had already posted my voice to silence. Now, my hands will stop talking. Words are worth the trouble when enchantment awaits us. Even if it is to cause us pain, as was the case with my love for Vastsome. But, now, I am incapable of any feeling. I have turned in upon myself, I am learning how to be a fortress. After writing so many lines, I know who I shall leave this letter to. To Marta Gimo. She was the last person to listen to me. Let it be her eyes to which I shall address my last word. Now, I am going to dream myself,

Tina

12 *Skyward once more*

That night, while Izidine was asleep, I was summoned by
the anteater. Suddenly exiled from my host, I returned to
my dead man's abode, lonely and deep. I took a few
moments to adjust my vision until the anteater hove into
view. The creature was curled up, as if asleep.

—*Me, sleeping? I wake up earlier than the dawn.*

The anteater unfurled itself. And then, without beating
about the bush, it came straight to the point.

—*You must agree, Ermelindo. This is all getting very
dangerous.*

The anteater tried to convince me to return once and
for all to my little hole. I should leave the world of the
living. And give them permission to declare me a hero.

—*Become a hero. They'll only disturb you from time to time.*

Dwelling among the living could only bring curses
down on me. The waterbuck died when he looked back
at his tail and wanted proof of what he was seeing. Stay
here, Ermelindo, be happy in your grave. Allow yourself to
be promoted to a hero's status. Even if it's a lie, need it
hurt you? Be like a porcupine. Isn't it its spines that give
the porcupine its peace of mind? And does a porcupine

ever prick itself with its own spines?

I sat down in my tomb. I picked up my old hammer. I beat the ground with it. No, I couldn't go back now. Was the world of the living a dangerous place? But I had already had a taste of what it might offer. Above all, I didn't have much time left on my pilgrimage through Izidine's body. Wasn't the policeman doomed? Weren't his days numbered?

And there was something else, too, something I couldn't confess to the anteater. It was the pleasure I got from being brushed against by a woman's existence. Marta Gimo gave me the illusion of returning to a time when I loved the woman of my dreams. In my grave I had no access to memory. I had lost the ability to dream. Now, lodged in the body of a living person, I could remember everything, everywhere, everytime. It was as if I were on my way back, on a return journey.

I could remember, for example, the noise of wood being struck. And it was as if I were now back in the time when I worked at the fort. In those days, when I was alive, I would busy myself first thing in the morning, turning timber into planks, squaring up windows, making doors into rectangles. One day – how I remember the day well – a group of men came up to me. They pulled at my shoulders and asked me aggressively.

—*Aren't you ashamed of building something to be used as a punishment for your brothers?*

Brothers? The ones they called my 'brothers' weren't related to me in any way. They were guerrilla fighters, revolutionaries. They were fighting the rule of the Portuguese. My heart wasn't in such conflicts. I had only ever been to a Catholic mission school. They had structured my ways, balancing patience with expectations. They had educated me in a language that wasn't my mother tongue. I lived under the eternal burden of being unable to match words with ideas. Later on, I learnt not to expect from the world more than my meagre destiny could provide. The only inheritance I received was poverty. Fear was the only present I was ever given. They should let me be, in that conformity.

But the other contract labourers pressured me with their demands. For example, they only pretended to be working. In fact, what they did was to cause problems, jam things up. I was the only one who took work on the prison seriously. And that's what they accused me of: I was working as a traitor, hangman of the righteous. I laughed in their faces. Let them try that argument in Jesus's case. Does anyone remember the carpenter who fashioned the cross? Does anyone blame him? No. The sinful hand belonged to him who nailed Our Lord's wrists.

—*Stop hammering or we'll hammer your scabby head.*

Does he who speaks give consent? I remained silent. I eyed those horny-handed bumpkins. They looked to me like spiders. Those huge spiders that shrivel up into nothing when dead. I smiled scornfully. One of them fanned me with threats.

—*Traitors pay for it. With you, it'll be with curses and fire.*

I went back to my hut. I shut myself away in total darkness, as was my custom. There was no cloth in my room. The door and curtains were made of wood: there wasn't a ray of light that could penetrate the gloom. That night, I could hardly contain myself. My eyes gazed into the distance to the point where they harvested ancient sadnesses. My eyelashes flooded, soaked with sorrows. But what was I crying for?

The following morning I went to the foreman. His wife attended to me and told me to wait. Her husband was still having his breakfast. But I was so anxious that I burst into his room. The man was perplexed by my plea.

—*Boss, I don't want to work at the fort any more.*

I made up a tattered excuse. That the sawdust had got into my chest. That I was like a miner, with my lungs open to the elements. Already I was coughing more than I was breathing. The fellow believed me. And transferred me to work on the beach. Down there, next to the rocks, they were building an anchorage. Before long, ships full of prisoners would put in there. They would only be able to moor there if the barrier of rocks could be tamed. Day after day, I joined planks together, increasing the surface of the land to form a pier. The whistle would be blown for work to stop and everyone would disperse. I alone would stay on to look at the sea, that gleaming terrace. It was there that I gained the comfort of an illusion: nothing in my life had been lost. Everything was like the ebb and flow of the waves.

It was round about that time that I began to get the strangest and gentlest of visitors. The first time I nearly died of fright. I was already asleep when I felt a hand touching me. Was I being attacked and my life disregarded? No, the intruder was favouring me with sugar-sweet caresses. I could feel its breath, unsettling the air. Lips wandered across my skin like fingers, as if spelling out my contours. Then it bit my neck. I couldn't work out who it was. No face offered itself to my acquaintance. Then its bulk came down on me, arms encircling my chest. It squeezed against my back, I could feel its roundness nestling up against me. Breasts, belly, buttocks. There's nothing in this world rounder than a woman's buttocks. Her body became my cradle, my outlet, my anchorage. My anonymous lover began to visit me frequently. After several boundless nights, I could taste my visitor on the tip of my tongue.

During the following days, I had only one thing on my mind: to guess who my night-time visitor was. For some time, I was convinced it was the foreman's wife. It wasn't just the recollection of her body that suggested this. It was, above all, her husband's nervous behaviour. Did the foreman suspect such passionate trysts? I would never know.

Once, the foreman's wife stopped me. She commented on my haggard look. Was I working too hard? Or was I taken up with affairs of the heart? The woman smiled mischievously. I stammered into the silence. She put me at ease: —*Don't worry, Ermelindo Mucanga, men always love what is not real, they pursue their fantasies of women.*

That night I waited anxiously for my visitor to arrive. I was now sure of her identity. I sensed her come into the hut and dissolve into the darkness. Her hands touched me, and I felt that familiar shiver electrify my body. I knew what was coming and offered my neck. I was waiting for her lips, her teeth, her tongue. The woman lingered in her caress. Until I felt her hot breath moistening my ear. That was when her teeth plunged violently into my flesh. What surprised me most was my own scream. I don't know whether anyone heard the other howls I failed to stifle. For this latest intruder, I discovered too late, was my executioner.

The only woman I had ever loved in my whole life had been a woman full of body but without a face. And I was afflicted by this uncertainty: could it be that in life I had loved a ghost? Was it not this that had killed me? And now, as a ghost myself, I was in love with a truly live being. That was Marta Gimo. The nurse gave shape to the visitor who had come to my hut at night. As if it had always been her, in all her perfections and imperfections. Marta reminded me of this figment of my imagination, intoxicating and brilliant. Like some subterranean creature, the memory was excavating another heart within my breast.

The anteater was now listening to my confession. Could he guess at the parts I had left out? The creature uncurled itself even more.

—*The choice is yours, my brother. Do you want to be a mole or a crab?*

The anteater was scared of losing my company. And it warned me —*You take care, Ermelindo: a heart that loves expands. But love grows more quickly than one's breast. Are your ribs big enough?* At that point, we argued. Who did the anteater think he was? He had so many years under his belt that his tongue was by now bigger than his mouth. When all was said and done, he was already losing his touch in matters of magic. The last time he came down to earth he had got into such trouble that he had lost a large number of scales.

—*That's nothing, it's the light that makes me unable to see.*

I was familiar with the *halakavuma*'s line of argument. We start learning about the world when we are still in our mother's womb. In the roundness of her belly, we learn to see even before we are born. The blind, who are they? They are those who had no time to complete their learning. As for the anteater's argument, I had known it by heart and back to front for a long time.

But in the hole that was my grave during my death, I was blind inside me. I couldn't really see my past, I had pretty much lost my memory. It wasn't that I was really unsighted. It was worse than that. I was like a dog that has lost its sense of smell. There are things we learn that distance us from the animals we really are. Such initiations are so hard that we no longer remember them. One thing we are pressed to forget, for example, is that among us humans, it is not the job of our teeth to bite. Through my strange woman visitor, I discovered that a tooth can, at one and the same time, be a razor and a piece of velvet. From that bite on the last night of my life, I had learnt death's final lesson.

I felt the weight of the hammer once more in my hand. The moment had come to make my choice: I was going to cross back into life, take refuge once again inside

Izidine Naíta. I had grown to like the young man, he contained a good dose of human kindness. I decided to go back to life with or without the *halakavuma's* permission.

Cycles +
Retrograded Causalities

13   Marta's confession

The culprit you seek, my dear Izidine, isn't a person. It's war. The war's to blame for everything. The war killed Vastsome. The war tore to shreds the world in which elderly folk could shine and had a role to play. These old timers who are rotting away here, were loved before the conflict. There was a world to welcome them, and families who put themselves out to care for the aged. Then violence brought other priorities. And the old were banished from the world, banished from we ourselves.

You must ask yourself why I stay on here, in this solitude. I always thought I knew the answer. Now, I have my doubts. Violence is the main reason for my retreat to this place. War creates another cycle of time. Our lives are no longer measured by years or seasons. Or by harvests, famine or floods. War establishes the cycle of blood. We start saying 'before the war, after the war'. War swallows up the dead and devours its survivors. I didn't want to be a relic of such violence. At least, here in the fort, the old ones tried to provide another kind of order in my life. They gave me the cycle of dreams. Their harmless ravings were the new walls of my fortress.

For a time I was still tempted by the city. And I even tried settling down there for a while. But I developed an illness that has no name. It was as if I were unlearning all my natural functions: listening, looking, breathing. There was a time when I thought I could change this world. But I've given up now for the world is a body that's alive thanks to its own sickness. It survives on crime and feeds on immorality. You, for instance, there in the police. Do you ever ask yourself how long it will take for you to be stricken by the sickness of bribery? You know only too well what I'm talking about: investigations that can be bought, policemen who accept backhanders. They took you off the drug-dealing case and transferred you to the narcotics section. Why? You know very well, Izidine. And why did they send you here, far from where the action is? Don't worry, I'll change the subject. Besides, I should be talking about myself.

Do you see that building over there, all in ruins? That was once an infirmary. That was where I worked. I would take delivery of medicines sent from the city. But the refuge was attacked, some weeks after I arrived. The gangs broke in here, robbed and murdered. They set fire to the infirmary. Two old women died. And if they didn't kill everyone, it was thanks to whom? Prepare yourself for a surprise, my dear Izidine. It was thanks to Vastsome Excellency. Are you amazed? Well, it was Vastsome who summoned up his courage and fought his way through the flames, saving the other patients. Only the charred walls of the building remained.

After the tragedy, I was left like those ruins. Above all,

when I found out that the main reason for the attack had
been me, Marta Gimo herself. The bandits wanted to
kidnap me and carry me off to their camp. It took time
for me to get over the incident. I never quite got over it,
though. War leaves wounds that no amount of time can
heal.

I asked Excellency for new stocks to be sent so that I
could set up the clinic again in my own room. By then I
had stopped sleeping under that roof. But there was no
room in the military helicopters that came and went.
There were other priorities, Vastsome Excellency told me.
I was denied the opportunity to reinvent myself. I would
have recovered if I had been able to rebuild the infirmary.

Without the clinic and any medicines, I was deprived
of a reason for living. You can't imagine how vital the
work in the infirmary was to me. It was my little hospital,
it was there I could dispense kindnesses. You should
understand: I was educated as a Portuguese. I'm from
Inhambane, it is many, many years since my family lost its
African names. I am the grand-daughter of nurses. The
profession reintegrated me into the family I had lost long
ago. Nor was the work in the infirmary easy. At first, I
almost gave up. I would go into a room and be hit by the
stench of putrefaction. I asked what the source of such
smells was. The old folk pointed to their open mouths.
The stench came from their pillows, from the nightly
dribblings of the toothless. I even believed it. Afterwards, I
saw it wasn't true. The smell came from the leftovers of
food they were hiding under their bolsters. They were
guarding these crumbs for fear of being robbed. The old

folk made up so many stories that sometimes they would invent food under their bolsters they didn't even get near to having.

Let me tell you something: those stories you're noting down in your book are full of untruths. These old people lie. And the more interest you show, the more they'll lie. It's been a long time since anyone made them feel important. One of the lies concerns Salufo, when they tell you he was loved by his family. It wasn't true. He pretended he had a lot of possessions just in order to be loved. Little Miss No made out she was a witch. So much so that she ended up doubting her powers. I also got over my lies, as if they were a skin that protected us, but that from time to time we had to shed.

A long time ago, before I came to this refuge, I was sent to a re-education camp. They carted me off to this camp charged with being a loose woman, as fast and slippery with men as with the bottle. None of my colleagues at the hospital stepped forward to defend me.

Today, I can tell you this much, inspector: life is like a cigarette. I only like the ash after the cigarette has been smoked. In the camp where I served my sentence, I debased myself through sex, drink and drugs. I didn't want to think of the future. I was only interested in the present moment. Flying doesn't depend on your wings. Doesn't the humming-bird, with its tiny wings, fly more perfectly than any other bird?

It was in such circumstances that Vastsome Excellency found me. He had power and influence, and got me out of there in return for my agreeing to work as a nurse at the refuge. That's how I came to be here, in this fort. At first, I was totally dispirited by this exile. Apart from the infirmary, I had nothing to occupy my time. So much so that I ceased to dream. I was only visited by nightmares. Whatever the organ is that secretes material for dreams, it was disabled. I was sick without having an illness. I was suffering from those fevers that God alone suffers. I'll tell you how it happened: first, I stopped laughing; then dreaming; and, finally, I lost the power of speech. Such is the order of sadness, the way despair imprisons us in a damp well. That's exactly what happened to Ernestina. Wait, and I'll get to her in a moment. I just want you to be aware of the inadequacy of my life at that moment.

It was because of such depression that I fell in love with Vastsome. Isn't love the most hopeless remedy? One day, he turned up and found me openly crying. He dried my face. I don't know whether you know the saying: he who wipes away a woman's tear will be bound by the knot of her handkerchief.

Vastsome and I began to meet at night. At first, he seemed to me as false as the blue that's used to describe the sea, but which you can never actually find there. But everything conceals elaborate secrets. I speak of water, not the sea. How can I ever know? The only ones who know the true colour of the sea are the birds, who look down on it from another realm of blue. Am I not explaining myself? It's that I came to know Vastsome, a man full of anguish, at a time when I myself felt crushed, embittered and belittled. Vastsome felt betrayed. He had given the best years of his life to the revolution. What

was there left of that utopia? In the beginning, aspects
that had divided us were disregarded. As time went by
they began to blame him openly on account of the
colour of his skin. His being a mulatto was the reason
for his forced exile. In his disillusionment, he began to
hate himself. He had a complex about his origins, his
mixed race. At that time it never occurred to me that,
when you think about it, we are all mulattoes. It's just
that in some cases, this is more visible on the outside.
Vastsome Excellency, however, had been taught to be ill
at ease within his own skin. He kept talking about other
people's race. And he had a preference for taking it out
on poor Domingos, so as to make it clear that he wasn't
giving whites any privileges. Wickedness became the
only way he could feel alive.

In spite of it all, I managed to love this man. I admit it,
don't be jealous. I desired him, yes, all of him, the sexual
being and the angel, the man and the child. Was he
handsome? What does it matter? I ask myself. Who cares
about beauty? It's life I want to touch in a man. That's
what I want. I want to feel tiny, a star in the sky, a grain of
sand. Correction: that's what I wanted. At that time, I still
saw men in the same way as birds are aware of a cloud:
somewhere one can pass through but never live in. But all
that was a long time ago, and I was still a girl. Vastsome's
courting was strange. Before touching me he would ask
me to weep. My tears would fall and he would lick them
as if drinking his last draught of water. It was the spring
that gave him courage. More than my own flesh. Now
that I no longer weep, I can understand Vastsome. It is our

tears that strip us bare. Our sobs reveal our most intimate nakedness.

Then I became pregnant. My body, in secret, declared itself the bearer of another body. I didn't want to tell anyone. I bore my belly furtively, no roundness was visible. But to my horror, Ernestina visited me one day and asked

—*So when is it due?*

I didn't know how to reply. Ernestina seemed not only privy to that secret, but to every other aspect of my private life. She looked deep into my eyes, but without any anger. Only a woman can look in that way. I wasn't even conscious of how my eyes looked. What did they appear to be saying when they stared at Ernestina? I spoke candidly, like a teenager admitting something to her diary, saying

—*I'm going to get rid of the child.*

—*How are you going to get rid of it?*

—*I'm a nurse, I know how to do it.*

And tight-lipped, I said no more. What words could I summon together, at that point? The director's wife leaned over me and her face was little more than a curse away from mine. Did Ernestina want to punish me for my folly? No. She simply knelt down and placed the palm of her hand upon my stomach. And so she remained, as if in a dream.

—*Is it so noticeable?* I asked.

—*I noticed it even before it happened.*

Then, frantic with sadness, she begged

—*Give the child to me.*

Ernestina grasped my hand. I sat for some time

without knowing what to think. No, there was no room
for hesitation: I had to terminate my pregnancy. I shook
my head to show her how impossible her request was.
Ernestina got to her feet solemnly, as if she had just
taken holy communion. I looked at her, full of fear. Even
before, I had noticed her strange behaviour. She used to
huddle for hours in the shade of the frangipani. Was she
praying? Was she talking with God? Or was she simply
postponing the pleasure of living? Long ago I too prayed,
I prayed a lot. Later I gave up. We pray so much, and yet
there are always more days than there are loaves of
bread.

On the next occasion, Ernestina surprised me again.
She had realised just how adamant I was in refusing to
become a mother. She walked round the room as if she
were looking for something. Then, she stopped in front of
me and began to unbutton her blouse.

—*Look!*

Her breasts challenged me in their fullness. She
paraded her beauty provocatively. She was exciting
herself, stroking her own nipples. Her hands wandered
over her breasts and down to her belly. Her fingers were
wooing herself. She came over to me and spoke in a low,
insinuating voice.

—*The child shall suckle here, at these breasts of a mulatto
woman.*

And just like that, without calming down, she left,
slamming the door behind her. After she'd gone, I was
speechless. The inside of one's mouth is always a shadowy
place. But I was in total darkness. I lingered on, my mind

wandering. Until, much later, Vastsome Excellency himself appeared. He wore a solemn expression. Before even greeting me, he said

—*I already know.*

Unlike Ernestina, he showed me no affection. The man was being evasive, opaque. Was he lying or was he now revealing himself just as he truly was? Does the dew fake pearls? Vastsome came to the point quickly. That telltale belly had to be put right as soon as possible. As he was the only fully functioning man, there in the refuge, suspicion would automatically fall on him. Indeed, who else could possibly be the culprit? Poor him, he might even lose his post along with all its rewards. I smiled disconsolately. Vastsome had jumped into the mortar but wanted to survive intact. Is it just that men are like that? Or is it merely that you can't have a nose without snot? Before I could stop myself, tears were flowing down my cheeks. I still thought Vastsome might lean over to drink my tear drops. But no. Never again would they be his spring of water.

Little Miss No visited me that night. She too already knew I was pregnant. The old woman had an angel's smile. —*Now, I no longer need rely on my fancy,* she said. —*I'm going to have a real child to suckle.*

And holding her arms like a cradle, she practised rocking a baby to sleep. I sat there with a blank, bewildered expression. My own state, Miss No's words, everything seemed unreal to me.

Little Miss No stayed on and fell asleep in her chair. Unable to control my inner life, I went around tidying things up until the witch awoke with a start. She shook her head, exorcizing a bad omen.

—*Don't have the child, don't have it!*

And without more ado, waving her arms about, the old woman shot off. I was left there, puzzled, at a loss to know what to think. When all was said and done, who was I to obey? Vastsome, whose only concern was for himself? Miss No and her bitter premonitions? Or Ernestina, who wanted to be the mother of another woman's child? On reflection, the fort didn't have the facilities for childbirth. On the other hand, I didn't want to leave the place either. I realised I had grown attached to it, the very place I had cursed so often. Out of habit, I had grown accustomed to accepting whatever happened, without ever provoking the wrath of the gods. Confused, incapable of taking a decision, I allowed my belly to shape its course.

This world is perfidious. Instead of Vastsome, I began to be visited by Ernestina. She brought me dishes and sweets she had prepared. She counselled rest and accompanying broths. It was as if the child were already hers, as if my belly were growing inside her own. I told her my doubts. There was still time to get rid of the foetus. She raised her hands to her face in distress.

—*No, don't do that.*

—*Don't do it*, she repeated, seizing my hands. I freed my arms and clasped her face. The woman was babbling ceaselessly, without even giving herself time to breathe. I had to raise my voice:

—*But Vastsome doesn't want this pregnancy.*

—*Vastsome doesn't have anything to do with the matter. The child you are carrying is mine. If you made love, it was with me, not Vastsome. Do you understand, it's our child, ours alone.*

Her words frightened me. I felt a terrible urgency to break free from that conversation. I was blunt.

—*Vastsome is the father. I must listen to his view.*

She came to her senses, as if she had been slapped. She hung her head, struggling with her thoughts until, sweeping the hair from her brow, she told me

—*If that baby dies, Vastsome will die too!*

I felt comforted by the force of those words. Ernestina didn't fill her mouth with false promises. She was no longer a broken woman. She had assumed a regal pose. With her newly-found dignity, she placed a hand on my shoulder and reassured me.

—*Don't worry. Give the child to me. I'll take him far away and give him a good upbringing.*

During the remaining months, I devoted every moment to perfecting my curve. The more moon-shaped I became, the more Ernestina raved with absurd utterances. She said she was going to be a mother too. She also took her protective vitamins. She did her breathing exercises in preparation for giving birth. And she sewed baby clothes. She would point at me and include herself.

—*We are both of us mothers!*

The unthinkable happened: Ernestina's belly also began to swell and curve. Was this a genuine pregnancy? Or was it the work of fancy? Where I come from, people usually ask: does one listen to a dog howling during the day? Vastsome gloomily waited for the first available helicopter.

He was going to export his obstinate wife. Ernestina
didn't react either way. The helicopter came and we both
caught it. We flew off to the city, where we were put in
different hospitals.

The night before the birth I was assailed by strange
visitations. The old folk from the refuge appeared to me
in a dream. They brought me frangipani flowers. They sat
round me as if at a wake. Little Miss No placed her hands
on my bed and told me the latest news.

—*Yesterday, the most terrifying thing happened at the fort.
The sky was suddenly covered with bats. The creatures flittered
and fluttered from the storeroom where Vastsome hid his goods.
These grey vampires, the colour of death, clouded the world. It
was like an eclipse. The creatures, baring their teeth and their
jaws, laid waste the houses. Their wings sounded like military
helicopters. The old people took shelter in panic. Then the bats set
about attacking the swallows. They devoured them in mid-air.
And so many of these tiny birds went to the slaughter that there
were red drops of blood everywhere. Their feathers quivered in the
air, falling softly to the ground. It was as if the clouds themselves
were shedding feathers. That day, it rained so much blood that the
sea became tinged with red.*

I woke up with the doctor at my side. He was holding
my hand and said

—*I'm so sorry! We did all we could.*

That night I had lost my baby. At the same time,
Ernestina was losing her second child. I looked at my
body, which had now lost its volume. Had the gods
answered my hidden wish not to be a mother? Suddenly,
there on the sheets, I saw something that startled me.

Next to me were the white flowers of the frangipani. And I fell asleep consoled by their perfume.

When I returned to the fort, everything was as I had left it. Vastsome's indifference. Ernestina's insanity. The tenderness of the old people who came out to meet me, as if I had in fact been elevated to motherhood. And I had to learn to hold back my tears when they began to call me 'mama'. Those same old folk taught me to recover from the wound that had ripped open both my womb and my soul.

Do you now understand the real reason why I sleep without a roof over my head? It's because, where I come from, women who are in mourning can only go to sleep in the open air. Until they are cleansed of death. But, in my case, there is no water with which to wash away the stain of death.

One day, somewhat recovered, I decided to go and see Ernestina. She had returned from hospital without being properly cured. During that time, she had lost the power of speech. Writing was her only means of talking. She shut herself away in her room, enveloped in darkness. Her only window was paper. The last of her letters is the one I gave you. I passed you that paper with the same feeling now as when I deliver these words of mine to you. As if I were unwrapping the clothes that cover our common child. Mine and Ernestina's.

14 The revelation

It was the last night. Marta came to call the policeman.
Her face brightened the gap in the doorway. She excused
herself.

—*Is it my turn to give a statement today?*

She didn't wait for him to answer. She walked over to
the inspector's chair and pulled him by the hand.

—*Come!*

She led him along the stone passage to her room.
Before opening the door, she turned suddenly. She kissed
him lightly. She brushed her fingers over his lips as if she
were branding her farewell on the surface of his flesh.
Then she opened the door. The old people were all
gathered in her room: Navaia Caetano, Domingos
Mourão, Little Miss No, Old Gaffer. The policeman went
in and walked forward while taking steps backwards.

—*What's happening?*

Mourão made a gesture with his hand, as if to suggest
he kept quiet. The witch got up. She was dressed for a
formal occasion. So was this it? The inspector supposed
himself to be in the middle of a ritual gazing into the
future. Little Miss No walked over to him and let

something slip from between her hands.

—*It's the last one.*

Izidine looked: it was another of the anteater's scales.
The witch told him to sit down. She swayed in front of
him, her eyes closed. After a while she said.

—*The* halakavuma *should really put in an appearance, and
fall from the sky up there.*

But nowadays, the creature no longer knew how to
speak the language of men. Little Miss No was mournful
—*Who told us to abandon our traditions? Now we have lost all
links with our messengers from heaven.* All that remained were
the scales left by the *halakavuma* on his last fall to earth.
Little Miss No had gathered them up next to the
termites' nest. They were the last relics of the anteater, the
very last feat pulled off by the great beyond. Each night,
one of those scales had worked upon the inspector's soul.
Now he was summoned to prostrate himself on the
ground right there, putting himself at the disposal of the
witch. She spread the anteater's scales over him: over his
eyes, on his mouth, next to his ears, and on his hands.
Izidine lay motionless, listening to the revelations which
followed. The stories mingled together, the old folk
speaking as if it had all been rehearsed. Miss No's words
rushed out in amongst her saliva. And she opened the
floodgates of her speech.

—*Do you know what the* halakavuma *does? The creature
rolls up and hides his belly, where he has no scales. Only at night
does he unroll, under cover of darkness. You, inspector must learn
to take such precautions. You should have developed ways of
prowling round here. But no. You frightened truth away. And what*

*are you doing now? Now you're like the bush pig that runs off
with its tail standing up. Be careful, inspector. In Maputo, you're
being hounded. Didn't they transfer you to another section?
Didn't they threaten you? Why don't you follow the lesson of the
scaly anteater? Why don't you curl up to protect your underbelly?
You don't know it, sir, but they hate you. You studied in the
white man's country, you've got the skills to face the manias of
the new way of life that has come since the war. The world that is
coming is your world, you know how to tread in the mud
without getting your feet dirty. They must wear the shoes of
falsehood and the socks of betrayal. The truth is this: you should
leave the police. You are a good fruit on a rotten tree. You are the
groundnut in a sack full of rats. They'll gobble you up before you
can cause them any discomfort. The problem is the pasture where
your colleagues graze. You don't know how pasture is made: it has
to be cut, not in order to kill it, but so that it will grow all the
stronger. We pity you because you're a foolish man. By this, I
mean you are a good man. You were pulled out of the pool where
the toads were, and you jumped into the one where the crocodiles
live.*

The words seemed to be emerging from her whole
body rather than just her mouth. She spoke in a
convulsive frenzy, spittle running down her neck. Until
the witch suddenly clasped herself, seized by a spasm.
Everyone was on tenterhooks, avidly awaiting the words
that were to follow.

—*Be careful! I see blood!*

—*Blood?* replied the policeman, alarmed.

—*They will come here. They will come to kill you.*

—*Kill me? Who is going to kill me?*

—*They will come tomorrow. You are already losing your shadow.*

Miss No's trance gathered pace. It was as if her body were being sparked into life by a bright flame.

—*It will be tomorrow. I can see the killer. It's the pilot. It's the same man who brought you in the helicopter. That's the one who's going to kill you. Not because he wants to. He's been given a mission: to remove you from this world. Izidine, Izidine: you've put yourself in a bees' nest. This fort is death's depository.*

And the witch, who was by this time breathing more normally, gradually peeled off the various veils which covered the director's mysterious death. There was only one true reason for the crime: the arms trade. Excellency had been hiding arms, left over from the war. They were kept in the chapel. Only Salufo Tuco had access to this storeroom. The fort had been turned into an arsenal. The old folk, at first, were unaware. Only Salufo knew about it.

Until, one day, the secret had emerged. And the old people, frightened, held a meeting. Those arms were the seeds of a new war. In the chapel, they were tending the burning coals of a hell which had already burnt everyone's feet. That was why they had decided to break open the depository at the dead of night and get rid of the weapons. They did this with Salufo's help. They had raised the idea of digging a hole. But Miss No had opposed it.

—*The earth isn't the place to bury arms.*

And that was why they had chosen to throw the arms into the sea. The boxes were tied to small rocks to give them the weight of eternal depth. They cast some in over

there, near the rocks. But the arms were too heavy for
their meagre strength. Apart from this, carrying boxes,
even under cover of night, attracted attention. The old
people had come to a dead end: they couldn't throw them
in the sea, and they couldn't bury them in the earth.
Where, then, could they get rid of this armoury? It wasn't
something that could be decided by process of thought.
Only Miss No's intervention could make it work. And
that's what happened. At a particular time, she turned to
the old timers and asked

    —*What is a hole that's lost its bottom?*

    —*It's nothingness itself.*

And the witch went on: it wasn't enough to throw the
arms out. There wasn't an outside big enough to
accommodate those death-stained weapons.

    —*What can we do then, Miss No?*

    —*Follow me, my children.*

And the witch led them over to the chapel. She opened
the doors with a mere brush of her fingertips. The old
folk watched Miss No's gesture, and even now can hardly
believe what they saw. She unfastened her *capulana* from
her shoulders and laid it down on the floor of the chapel.
From a bag she took out a chameleon and made it walk
across the cloth. The reptile changed colours, rotated its
eyes and started to swell. It puffed itself up like a ball.
Suddenly, it burst. It was then that the world rumbled and
rolled, and all the darkness in the clouds overflowed. The
old folk coughed, waving away the dust with their hands.
Before their very eyes, they beheld something fantastic
happen: there, where the ground had been, was a

bottomless hole, the entrance to emptiness itself, a hollow within a void.

They immediately got to work, and threw the arms into the depths. They emptied the weapons into the abyss and remained, for an infinity, listening to the noise of metals clashing with each other. To this day, arms can be heard echoing through the void, emptying away beyond the world.

Then one day, the helicopter returned. It was coming to fetch the arms. A group of uniformed men climbed out of the chopper and went to the storeroom. The old people stood watching from a distance. The strangers opened the door to the storeroom and some of them marched straight to the chasm, abruptly stopping inside the entrance to that desolate place. The others retreated in astonishment. Who had dug such a trap? And where were the arms?

A heated argument began. They were suspicious of Vastsome. They took him inside his house. After only a few moments shots were heard. They had killed Excellency. They brought his body out and threw it onto the rocks by the beach.

—*It was they who murdered Vastsome Excellency. It was them, the same people who are going to kill you, inspector. Tomorrow, they're going to come and kill you.*

Little Miss No finished speaking and fell to the ground, exhausted. Izidine Naíta left the ceremony, went to his room and wrote all night long. He wrote down his thoughts like God: straight but without guidelines.

Whoever read him would have the task of disentangling his words. In life, only death is precise. The rest balances between the two shores of doubt. Like poor Izidine: pen in his right hand, pistol in his left. The policeman was losing his coordination. He nodded off on the table, his head cushioned by the sheets of paper. He fell asleep.

He awoke, startled by a sound from the door. He jumped up and pointed his gun. It was Little Miss No. She was carrying a rusty tin. The witch went over to him in silence. She unbuttoned his shirt. She plunged her fingers into some yellowish grease and began to spread it on him.

—*I'm rubbing this whale oil into you.*

Miss No talked as she massaged Izidine's chest. —*The whale is large, and you will become bigger beyond measure. They will cast you onto the waves. They will think that nothing will remain of your body, torn apart in its encounter with the rocks. But death will no longer be able to take you in its embrace. You will be as slippery as fire. The waves will bear you away to a place where no boat will find you. There where the sea flows into the rivers. Where palm trees are planted in the waves, and take root deep inside coral reefs. You will turn into a water spirit and you will be greater than any voyage. I, Little Miss No, water-woman, tell you this. You will be the one who dreams and doesn't question its truth. You will be the one who loves without wishing to know whether it is lasting.*

Izidine Naíta couldn't see it but I, the spirit inside him, watched the witch even after she had closed the door behind her. She left, like one with guilt on her conscience. She walked with her eyes on the ground and then stopped. She looked at the tin with which she had blessed the policeman, turning it in her hands. She shrugged her shoulders and then threw the tin away.

15   The last dream

Little Miss No's discouraging gesture caused me to reach a decision. I was set to abandon the inspector's body. I couldn't allow that young man to die, sinking into a destiny that had already been revealed to me. I preferred to suffer the sentence of the grave, even if I were to be subjected to being promoted as a false hero.

That morning, I left Izidine Naíta's body. I would drag the remains of my worldly matter along with me, a ghost only visible from the front. The strong light of day filled me as soon as I disembodied myself from the policeman. At first, everything sparkled in a thousand glimmers. The light gradually tamed itself. I looked at the world, everything around me was coming into existence. And I murmured to myself, my voice soaked in emotion

—*This is my land, my own land!*

Though downtrodden and dusty, it struck me as the only true place in the world. My heart hadn't been buried after all. It was there, always had been there, reappearing in every new flowering of the frangipani. I touched the tree, picked a flower, breathed in its perfume. Then I wandered along the terrace, the ocean courting my gaze. I remembered the anteater's words

—*This is where the land and time retires to sleep.*

I began to hear the rotor blades of the helicopter. I was seized by confusion. They were here! Everything in me speeded up. I heard the voice of the *halakavuma*.

—*Go and get the young man.*

While I ran, the words of the anteater rang through my head. The *halakavuma* was telling me his plans. He would assemble the forces of this and other worlds, and would unleash a storm to beat all storms. Hail and lightning would pound down upon the fort.

During these terrifying events, I should just follow his instructions.

—*You pilot the boat, and I'll drive the hurricane.*

The boat? What boat? Or was it just an image without an enigma? But the anteater had already fallen silent. I ran to Izidine's room and called him.

—*Quickly, come this way! They've arrived.*

At first, the fellow was suspicious of me, confused and bewildered.

—*Who are you?*

There was no time to explain. I yelled my command: he was to follow me. The policeman still hesitated for a moment. Then he looked up at the sky and recognised the impending threat. At that point, he decided to hurry after me. We ran towards the beach. The helicopter chased us, hunting like a vulture overhead. I led Izidine onto the rocks, where we would be able to take cover. When we threw ourselves down among the boulders, I looked at myself in shock. And I thought to myself: I had lived a life of lies. I had crowned myself with cowardice. When it was time to fight for my country I had refused. I had nailed planks when some were building the nation. I was loved by a shadow when others were multiplying themselves with living bodies. While alive, I hid myself from life. When I was dead, I hid myself in the body of a living person. And when my life was genuine, it was a lie. Death hit me with such truth that I couldn't believe it. Now was my last chance to move in concert with time. And to help deliver a world in which a man could be respected just for living his life. After all, isn't it the anteater who says that all creatures are as ancient as life itself?

All these thoughts were parading through my mind when, suddenly, the storm burst. It was like something never witnessed before: the whole sky caught fire, the clouds blazed and the world became as hot as a furnace. All of a sudden, the helicopter went up in flames. Its blades became detached and the machine, now wingless, fell like one of those scraps of paper that, when alight, don't know whether they're losing or gaining height. And so the machine, enveloped in tongues of fire, crashed onto the roof of the chapel. It came to grief on the exact spot where the arms were kept. It was then that a huge explosion shook the entire fort, and it was as if the whole world had been set ablaze. Thick clouds darkened the sky. Gradually, the smoke dispersed. When all was light once more, there appeared from that bottomless pit thousands of swallows, filling the firmament with sudden points of brightness. The birds flashed over our heads and scattered over the blue hills of the sea. In an instant, the sky gained wings and fluttered away, far from the world.

Then I saw the old people approaching us along the beach. They were supporting each other. Behind them came Marta. Izidine Naíta urged me to go and join them to help. I couldn't. Like I said, a spirit within a real living body can't touch another living being, for if it does, it will inflict death.

Everyone, the old timers, Marta, Izidine and I, met under the platform which, strangely, still remained over the rocks, that same quay which I had shaped and nailed together when I was alive. The covering was resistant and sheltered us from the rain and fire. The structure which had been designed to hasten the killing of prisoners now served to protect my living companions.

Little by little, the sky was cleansed until it was so translucent that other firmaments could be seen beyond the blue. When, finally, everything was calm, a silence reigned as if the entire earth had lost its voice.

—*Did you see the helicopter?* Izidine asked excitedly.

—*What helicopter?*

The old witch burst out laughing. What the policeman had taken for a flying machine was the *wamulambo*, the storm snake. And the others all joined in her laughter. Little Miss No ordered them to return to the fort. She took the lead and opened a path among the places that had caught fire. What a shock I got: as we advanced, the ruins turned back into perfect walls, the buildings re-emerged intact. Were the fires I had seen and the explosions I had witnessed no more than figments of my imagination after all? But amid all that remained, there was proof of the recent chaos, a witness to the destruction visited upon that place. It was the frangipani tree. All that was left of it was a crude skeleton, fingers of charcoal embracing a void. Its trunk, leaves, flowers, all had been reduced to ashes. The old people slowly reached the terrace and took care not to tread on the charred remains. Sidimingo couldn't believe his eyes.

—*Is it dead?*

The sight of that death reminded me of my own end. My turn had come to re-enter my shadow once more. I waved sadly to the old people. I took my leave of the daylight, the voices, the moist morning air. I began to descend into the sand, ready for darkness again. But in the middle of it all, I hesitated: my return journey could not be like this, for that soil no longer accepted me. I had become a foreigner in the kingdom of death. Now, in order to cross the final frontier, I needed to do it clandestinely. How would I cross over, while still deathbound?

I recalled the teachings of the anteater. The tree was a place of miracles. So I got down from my body, and touched the ashes, turning them into petals. I turned over the remains of the trunk, and the sap, like the earth's semen, began to flow once more. With every gesture I made, the frangipani become reborn. And when the tree was fully restored, newly born into the fullness of life, I covered myself with the same ash into which the plant had disintegrated. In this way I let myself enter plant life, preparing for my own arborescence. I was waiting for the final stage of my transformation when a tiny thread of a voice halted me in my tracks.

—*Wait, I'm going with you, my brother.*

It was Navaia Caetano, the old man–child. Time had already confiscated his body. He was leaning against the trunk, losing the natural colours of life. He was insistent.

—*Please, brother!*

He was calling me brother. The old man was confirming my human state, without blaming me for having been anything else. Holding out his hand, he asked me

—*Touch me, please. I want to go too . . .*

I held his hand. But then I noticed he had his toy hoop over his shoulder. I asked him to leave the useless thing behind. Metal was forbidden over there. But then I heard the anteater's voice correcting me.

—*Let the plaything in. It's not as if this is the last time . . .*

And Navaias's face lit up in childish delight. He clutched my hand and together off we went, into our own shadows. Just as my body was in the final stages of disappearance, I looked back and noticed the other old people were going down with us, bound for the depths of the frangipani tree. And I heard Ernestina's gentle voice, lulling a distant child to sleep. On the other side, bathed in light, stood Marta Gimo and Izidine Naíta. Their image was fading, all that remained of them was a double crystalline halo, the brief glint of dawn.

Little by little, I am losing the language of men to take on the earth's dialect. Up there, on the terrace, bathed in its luminosity, I bequeath my last dream, the frangipani tree. I am merging with the sound of stones. I lie down, more ancient than the earth. From now on, my slumber will be deeper than death itself.

CPSIA information can be obtained at www.ICGtesting.com
Printed in the USA
LVOW11s0704010215

425020LV00001B/1/P